BE-BOP, RE-BOP

Cover design by Bill Toth
Book design by Iris Bass
Photo credit: Kwane Shauku

BE-BOP, RE-BOP

XAM WILSON CARTIÉR

AVAILABLE
PRESS

BALLANTINE BOOKS • NEW YORK

An Available Press Book

Library of Congress Catalog Card Number: 87-91229

ISBN 0-345-34833-8

Manufactured in the United States of America

First Edition: September 1987

10 9 8 7 6 5 4 3 2

For the vision of Albert Wayne Wilson & the memory of Hannibal Cleveland Carter, and for all my other supports—Mary Carter Wilson, Kristin, Amanda, Nell L, Baraka, Brooks, Reed, Rasul, Ghasem, Jan, Yon, Melody, Mary Mo (oh don't you know?), MLS, S&Q, RL, RA, BR, CW, CB, AMT, CC & all the rest of the bumped-out goodcompany, jammin up a squared off storm!

We just play *Black*.
We play what the day recommends.

—Miles Davis

I

Double or Nothing and All That Jazz!

Be-Bop, Re-Bop & All Those Obligatos

The liquor was flowing, everyone had a plate, folks had visited all the way back to the kitchen. . . . We were just settling into the spirit of Double's funeral wake when Vole took it in mind to drive all the guests from the house.

For some reason of crisis insanity and because my first reaction to mayhem is to staple down the madness to some detail of order, I've begun to take stock of the folks in the room, to estimate the number of floating mourners who've made their way past the living room rut to the recondite sanctum in the rear of the house. There are twenty-four people poised at candid angles as far back through the room as the eye can see, including five men: two family friends and three co-workers of Double's whom I've seen two or three times. The women, role models around me, are fine-feathered birds flown from flighty Saks and Montaldos, the *haute couture* rooms. We're all, all of us are musing over inscrutable chalices of highballs, including me in spasmodic sweet-sixteenhood, thanks to the blessing of mother-gone-from-the-room, but now Vole's back, so here's my solo, about to be crimped. . . .

Vole had been resting in the bedroom away from it all when Mona threw out, "Some folks might've called him irresponsible and impulsive, but one thing about Double is, he might have been practically back down to where he started when he died, but now there was a man who could keep going when the chips were down no matter *what* it took. If it took a Tom, he'd be one, and he has his own good reasons too, he must have, considering what he stooped to just to hold on to that trifling job in parcel post. It was the best thing he'd ever lucked up on."

She sucked her teeth and shook her head.

"Truth is the light," somebody said.

"Let it shine," somebody else said.

"Now *some* folks might have said Double was a dreamer with no firm sense of direction;" Mona went on, "they'd have said he was good for nothing but dead-end dreams . . . but I know better! though Double *had* him some dreams, at least til Vole started to stay on his back—she rode him all the time you know, though let it be said, Double needed some get-up and go. Don't talk about the dead, but youall know what I mean, you can't live a man's life for him; you've got to let him breathe. Vole knows that— maybe she's got another opinion—but well, you all know the story: You don't miss your water til your well runs dry!"

She raised her glass to the tune of the assents around her.

"Well, well, well." Vole appeared in the doorway looking store-rack crisp in her undefiled black dress, faille skirt riding impossible curves of her paragon legs. She raised that tight tan face, angled those high-carved cheekbones, fast-focused those radar eyes from their dusty socket-shadows. Her fingers draped the knob of the door like a mannequin's hand but for the fingernails, which she trimmed stoically in ruthless crescents. We're all looking over at her, ruffled in our own different ways, with reactions ranging from bitterness to outrage. Where are Vole's tears anyway? I'm thinking—and where's the crash of her gloom? There she stands, intact and unacceptable as usual. Her sometime pal Mona is one juror in particular who gives Vole the eye; Mona's response to Vole at the moment is disappointment that the convicted widow's alive and well.

"Having fun?" Vole flings at Mona over under-musical silence and rustling nudges, just as Mona's in process of leaning her emerald suede vested chest toward the woman beside her, in bracing gesture of *uh-oh*. . . .

"Now Vole, just calm down, honey," Mona dodges, the defense is pushed out of her instantly and she rolls on automatically: "Death is always hard, we know that, and it's hardest on the widow, yes, it always is, it's the shock, and—"

"What do you know?" Vole cut her off at the pass of her sass. "Just what in the *hell* do you know?" And

I tense, since I feel Vole building to an open storm of her closet feelings; already she's lapsed into what she calls *vulgar language in public*, brazenly defying the Salt Away Box (this being a cylindrical empty salt box that we keep family fines in; whoever cursed had to pay). "I'm tired, but I ain't crazy," Vole goes on with further indication of no-holds barredness, her lapse into "slang" as she calls it. "I'm tired but I ain't crazy enough to think you actually give a damn about anybody's grief, least of all mine, or do I *look* like a fool? Tell me anything!" Vole's leaning forward now with arms crossed across her chest, a hanging judge, waiting. . . .

"Uh—" starts Mona. . . .

"Yeah, 'uh,' " says Vole relentlessly, leaning further toward defendant— "Come on, tell me anything, just front me right off. I'm supposed to be under the influence of widowhood, so you can't go wrong. Come on, don't let me stop your show since you know so much. Knock yourself out, come on; make like I'm not here.

"Look at you," Vole sneers on, "in your weep motif. You never did a damn thing for Double while he was alive, or for any of the rest of us" (here she gestures maternally toward me), "and you know it. But you take plenty time to rake us through with your mouth, mouth almighty, fatmouth queen, brilliantine—"

("God*damn*" goes someone's hushed catharsis; all of us onlookers had been swept into the spirit of Vole's testimony)—

"Well surprise, fools"—Vole turns to the room at large—"I can read you like a book. But don't let that throw you—" With this last you can hear a crew of

6

voices arming with mumbles for self-defense just in case, be prepared, but look! There's Vole, on everyone's case already . . . here she comes, snatching plates of food and drinks from visitors ("Here, I'll take that"), rushing out of the room mechanically, then back again now with armloads of hats and coats which she flings in a heap on the couch and returns for the rest.

"If it took a Tom, he'd be one. . . ." It's this I consider during the following frantic interval; I try not to, but can't help but think it, this peanut butter thought that sticks to the roof of my immature mind . . . I think of the time only last week, when Double had lost his post office gig and Vole and I had passed him talking on the wallphone in the hall. . . .

"Well, do you take colored?" Double had mouthed this then in mealy manner, or so it seemed to the both of us, Vole headed one way and I another, so that *What?* we stop and stare at each other, then both jump in at once—

"Do they do what?" Vole challenges Double and then walks away with no further display, a mystery to teenage me at the time, and I stay on to follow her words with a cop-bust frown of disgust aimed at Double, this at know-all black-and-white stage of analysis development, righteous adolescence. To tom or not to tom—seemed perfectly clear to me. . . .

Aw Double, I thought at the wake then that day, there it is, so my hump of shock and let-down can sink to its rest in the pit of my stomach—Was our case really so critical then that we were all the way down to our tommery? I asked myself again and

7

again all through that week, near the time of your seemed-to-be sin when I thought I knew the answer, one answer: *Hell no! You can be down to death, and not down to tom!* Yet—this I know now—what could you do, standing limp with livelihood soon to be lost, as you knew, to the rake of unfeeling circumstance? What's more I'm human too and've whipped out my own slave-kerchief in time of distress, "It's reflex survival," I fibbed to myself until then when that day at your wake all your contrivance (just venial conniv-ance, not mortal!)—all your contrivance comes flood-ingly clear and wet comprehension, it courses a trail through the heat of my face.

Militant memories: For months, years after his pass-ing Double would appear through my sleep to bump a lesser dream, still bopping with the armed resis-tance of his dedication to "jazz"— which he said was "two, say three broad crooked jumps off to the side of the mainstream straight and narrow, out to where sound becomes sight, as it should be!"

When I think of Double that day at his wake, I see him standing beside the radio with his forefinger crooking for me to run over and check out this riff or those taps or that vamp or these changes. This I'd casually stroll up to do with cool beyond my childish years; my thumbs would be tucked in pinafore straps under fat kinky braids that laid on my chest.

"*And how's Daddy's masterpiece comin along?*"

"*Aw, I can't kick.*"

"*Well say hey, whatcha know?*"

"*Aw, you got the go!*"

"*So tell me, what's to it?*"

"Nothin to it but to do it!"
"Mean to say YOU can do the do?"
"Can Ella Fitz cut a scat? . . . . Then, don't hand me that!"
"Can Eisenhower dance? Say HEY—not a chance!"
"Hey now. And how!"

My smallfry face at Double's knee. Abracadabra afternoons! And every day, on the way home from kindergarten at BookerTWashington School, there's hopeful harmony of Double and me, two hipsters vocaleesing to wide-angle sound up front in the Studebaker.

"Oop bop shabam, buh do be do,
We like to boogie, woogie, re-bop and be-bop it too!"

Yet Double has died. But why call it *death*, when in the scheme of simple reality, I should be and am convinced by the age of sixteen (time of no questions) that his passing, like his music, is more process than product by nature—that Double's demise has the matrix-free flow of an on-the-spot bop change. So since I know he's still bopping nearby in time to the tune of temporality, while Vole's handing out the coats and hats at his wake, I shake the scheme of my dream and seize the opportunity to come up with a note of relevant reality for the mourn-watchers.

"A side of Fats, anyone?" I call out, surrounded by scotchsippers' eyebrows jumping like spastic grasshoppers. "Ain't Misbehavin" has popped into mind like the miracle of the gramophone. So *apropos!* Talk about chromatic consciousness—why it's the final flipside! Besides, it was Double's favorite jam, so I put it on the hi-fi and turn it to crescendo. Then's when Vole turns to face me so suddenly that distress bends distended in our corner of the cosmos—rapport needs no words in light of the sight of Vole rushing toward me with her hand upraised, the hand which she uses to spin me in place for a heartfelt lindy hop, steps of which I fall into by rote due to Double's diligent teaching—and Vole and I, hey, well we dance past all woe for a whirlaround while!

Double or Nothing and All That Jazz

Double's death was a personal nuclear disaster that radiated negative energy in all directions, from was-peaceful past to fallout-filled future. For one thing, death hit Double so all of a sudden that it seemed too contaminating to absorb. I found myself starting to envy folks whose folks had died of lingering cancer or any other dress-rehearsal disease; at least they'd had a fair cool-down period: Death had said *All right, here's the cue for my solo,* and the grieved-to-be had been able to say, *"Goddamn! Why him?"* til they wore themselves out in a natural way. All their guilt and blues had had a chance to sift around til it settled in place, not like me and my lump that still pulsates, oozing poison gas at random.

Yet Double/dear Papa was dead all right—though

his death began my siege of dreaming for months, years after his passing that he still was standing beside the chifforobe with one foot resting on the radiator, singing the "Monkey Song" as I called it in kidhood, about one of the world's perennial agitators, this one anthropoid and clinging to the back of a wily buzzard who, pragmatist that he was, was bent on devouring the monkey dead or alive.

. . . Loosen up, said the buzzard,
you're chokin me. . . .
Loosen up your grip .
and I'll set you free.

The monkey looked the buzzard
right dead in the eye:
"Your story's very touchin—
but I know it's a lie!"

When I think of Double, I hear him tapping his feet in time to the beat of developing melody, humming or scat-singing, winging his way through music of process, running through tonal tongue-to-tooth changes with curled fingers striding, flying off ivories in thin air. He'd turn to me in mid-riff with a question in the movement of his eyebrows—

"Young Fats," I'd answer with head cocked to doubledare side. "Young Fats, early Stride!"

Then came a pause, and next, his applause for diligent growth on the part of a smallfry. *"Whoo-whee! The kid's on the ball! What say? SKIN me, my friend!"*

And I'll do it again! I'm kneehigh at the time and filing the bulk of Double's sagacity for future refer-

12

ence, though already I've soaked up weight enough to hold my own in our name-that-tone champion finals. Fact is, I'm still spongy with pride when Double takes me aside to show me a dog-eared copy of a nineteenth-century abolitionist's knotted dialectic on the "marvelous complication" and "curious rhythmic effect" of a "strong musical network" which defied all due deployment of whitefolks' wit.

"See?" Double said then. "They never can manage to hook up our music to its source in the ghetto, be it concrete or cotton. Their bright idea has always been to rip up our music and chop it off at the roots, grimreaper style, just like they do their turnips. They keep the leaves and scrap the soul of the taste in the turnip!"

Our music. It's Double's top doctrine. And by default and devotion, I'm his ace apostle. Which's why later that same afternoon near the noon of it all, when Double's working his graveyard shift so's my daily caretaker while Vole social works her days away, Double and I've been jitterbugging up a storm all over the front room and now we're seated respectfully on the throw rug in the corner, watching the combination radio, a dome-shaped mahogany Mahal for the sounds coming through. We're as intent as if we can see through to the carrier crystal inside the box, major and minor soul-sensors that we are— watching as if the animated armoire is a t.v., which is further down the line of dreamed-up illusion. But movement seems to materialize suddenly from the radio bowels, and a wildroot-dampened lilliputian, dapper ofay dollhouse doll, steps up to a miniature microphone between two fat black vacuum tubes.

"You said it!" he enlightens, as we look on un-amazed. "That was *Scrapple From The Apple!*" Then he turns to flash a bright white turnip smile at all of us here in the jimcrow balcony.

But look! Here comes wonder-worker Ladyday, tipping onstage from the wings, wearing her wiltless gardenia and sizzling sequins and mellow phantom pain, pulling free for a while from her private prison with grief disguised as a series of croons:

. . . *I don't stay out late* . . . (Yeah, Billie!) . . . *don't care to go* . . . *'m'home about eight* . . . *just me an my ray-dee-oe* . . .

She knocks us out. Kills us. Absolutely! And Double's now in process of snatching me up into a topheavy foxtrot, with his scratchy cheek to cheek. . . . We're riding out on a riff, right on up to the rickety railing in the redbrick hallway, don't-give-a-damn gliding right on down to the front door with its held-back reality demons. Then back we swing toward the tune, in a serious gravity sweep to the source. A dip; we part. Brief shadow of a simple separation.

Why is it that time is so upbeat discreet, cuts no slack in its tempo for our schemes unredeemed? The illusion of endings in this world. Addictive fantasy.

Wait, Time, don't you see? At just 43 he was kicked into infinity by an off-the-rack/black/heart attack/and I was only/I'm still trying to improvise/to finishingtouch-up the rest of his life/in the riffs and the runs (BOPBOP/A-REE BOP!) of the chase through the (BOOGEDY/BOOGEDY/ BOPBOPBOP) neo-blue/everblack/labyrinth life

of my dreams!

A Matter of Taste

According to norm and nevermind Hoyle, Double had cooked dinner such as it was—canned lima beans (a gruesome family favorite to my kid's taste at the time), fried chicken which he'd paprikaed down in spots where the brown was missing, thick beige gravy, canned spinach: dark green and the top of it sprinkled with shocking yellow and white boiled egg pieces for contrast in the spirit of Double's aesthete's touch, and canned dairy-case rolls: innocent looking fakes with a telltale smell.

To date I'd lost weight to the size of a child two years younger and two-thirds as tall as myself, according to the chart painted on the pediatrician's scale where I did my on-the-spot research while waiting for the doctor to come and check me over. I remember being called upon to explain my weight loss—afterall, I'd been getting enough to eat yet here I was in bold sad shape, the upstanding child of a mother who could articulate the doctor to shame—and me just standing there thinking, inwardly test-running my tale of excuse since it beat me too, I knew I was to blame, but *Give me time enough*, I'm thinking: *I'll come up with something.* . . . Which's when the doctor decrees that to spark my appetite I only can have milk at the end of my meals, a diabolical punishment tailor-made to fit. Milk is my favorite food, and I use it religiously as a sacrosanct supplement to everything on my plate.

But after we'd eaten dinner that day—Double'd had to get up repeatedly to round up Muz from the bedroom where she'd retreated time and time again during the course of our meal; she'd take a bite of spinach and stray away mysteriously with no explanation, to take care of business of her own, apparently mental—she had to get her worrying done, it seemed; I couldn't tell at the time. At any rate, after dinner Double was on his way to the bedroom with a dish of ice cream for Muz, his beloved Vole, who was off to herself again by this time, sequestered once more. The ice cream was vanilla, her favorite, with chocolate sauce on top. I just had dug down into my own bowl of it—in those days we all were ice cream junkies driven by fumbling nutrition-hunting instinct—when I decided to creep up to the door of their room so as to lay in wait for Double's return. When he appeared, I'd planned to startle him with all my might just on general principles, a kid's priorities. So there I was in the hall, flattened against the wall near the door with my dish of ice cream setting on the floor beside me, when I heard Vole say in quick-severed silence, ". . . so what's this you've brought me, the consolation prize?"

Then I could hear Double's careful drawl, "You . . . think . . . of the damndest things!"

"You think of the damndest answers," said Vole. "Now come up with one for this mess that we're in!"

"Look," Double said. "How do you think it makes *me* feel? I'm used to pullin my own weight around here!"

"Well buddy," said Vole, "the full load just shifted to my side of the wagon. So you'd best to manage those reins with all your spunk!"

"I'm workin on it!"

"He's working on it," Vole sighed. "What a relief!"

"Well what do you expect me to do? I can't just rush in and—"

"Heaven forbid you should *rush*!"

"Just what am I suposed to do? Answer me that!"

"You can protest it, that's what! How many times do I have to tell you—"

"That's what *I* want to know!" Double sliced in. "How many times can I look forward to hearin this same jack again and again? I mean how many times can we go round the mulberry bush and still stay sane?"

Vole stopped for a moment; she had to regroup or recoup her lost lather before she continued pursuit of the issue.

"When are you going to confront this thing and deal with it?" she said, straight ahead. "If you're waiting for a cue, *here*! Take this one!"

"I told you, I'm waitin til—"

"The man's '*waiting*,' " Vole said in a weird tone of awe.

" 'You stand when it's *time* to stand!' Remember that line?"

"That was an entirely different situation!"

"Was it?" said Double. "What do you take me for? I'm not go' let a clown like Crimshaw badmouth me, call me outa my name, get all up in my face an get away with it. I should've jumped down his throat on the spot—but naw!" He shook his head heroically. "What makes you so sure I'm way off base, when you don't even know what happened?"

"I know what's happened." Vole jerked to face Double. "What's happened is from now on, every Friday your paycheck will be missing in action from the post office roll, and nine years of seniority's washed down the drain in a matter of indiscreet minutes!"

"Ain't that a scream?" Double said as if to himself. "I was '*indiscreet*'? How do you think I got suspended from duty? You think I lost some kind *manners* competition? Well I want you to know, Emily Post wasn't at the scene of the shit—an if she hadda been there, she wouldn't of given a hot hump in hell!"

"There's no need to be crude," Vole said with disgust. "Use your head instead of your heart for one solid second. Try it on for size! What I'm saying is—Man, this is like pulling teeth!—What I'm tryin to get across to you is the simple fact that there's an established line of recourse for a situation like this." She stopped for a while to stockpile strained patience. "There's such a thing as a grievance hearing. All you have to do is file a formal complaint. Just take your case to the grievance committee. That's what they're there for!"

"Yeah, *solid!*" Double said with weird late elation. "Sure thing. Take it up with Crim's Klan pals at the top. Thanks for the tip!"

"You don't know that," Vole said. "You don't know a thing about that white man! So don't start cooking up hold-me-backs to stop yourself before you get started!"

"You must think I'm a full-fledged fool," Double said in a terminal tone. "Be for real! If I take this thing up with the brass in the office . . . Hell, Crim's their main boy! He does their biddin an then some. They love his dirty draws!"

"There's no need—"

"If I turned the searchlight on Crim, they'd go ahead and fire me so fast it'd make your head swim."

When he went into work at three A.M. that morning, it had been like any other day— He spotted Aldrich first off as usual, short, chunky Aldrich practicing postal zone schemes, sorting a stack of 3X5 cards and pitching them into the wood slatted envelope rack as fast as he could.

Across the room was lanky, slap-happy Sky Chief, hanging up his coat at the locker. ("What's up, man?" "Aw, sky's the limit!") And down near the time clock was long Arvis. ("Hey Arvis, what you know good?" "Ask me again at 12 o'clock noon.") And here—just follow the scent of the Maxwell House—was P.Q., with his freckles and grin.

"Hey, hey, cool Papa," Double said, "tell me somethin slick."

"Old Crimshaw won't be in today," said P.Q. "He got hit by a truck and dragged fifty miles on a new-tarred road."

"On the level?"

"Naw, but I can dream, can't I?"

And yeah, bringing up the rear of the ranks as the men filed into the mailroom beyond was red-eyed Too Short Perkins, always late ("Thass cuz I got places to see an women to do"). . . . And up ahead, with his hostile cigar chewed to a sorry state of disaster was old tightjaw Crimshaw with his narrow pink self, lookin at his watch and smilin that same slippery smile.

"Step right in, boys. We're all waiting for you." He *pointed to a hill of overstuffed mailbags at the warehouse end of the room where five or six black handlers worked, heaving five-foot sacks from truck to loading dock.* "Hey, *budd. You, pal."* Crimshaw grinned at Double. "Go give *em a hand. On the double."*

Double waited for a moment, undecided.

"Get the lead out, boy. Hop to it!"

The other men had begun to fan forward in different directions, dragging sacks to their posts at the sorting racks.

"Thought you didn't want me workin parcel post," Dou*ble said to Crimshaw who was walking toward the trucks.*

"I want you working where I want you working." Crimshaw turned and grinned. "You got any objection to *this job?"*

"Not if it's got no objection to me—" Before he could *think he had said it, and still he didn't know what had happened next. Too Short said that Crimshaw pushed the loaded mail cart at Double on purpose—he had to brace his shoulders against it and shove it with his foot to get it to roll at that speed. Aldrich said Crimshaw tripped and fell onto the cart so couldn't stop himself from crashing into Double before Double jumped and slammed it back at Crim. P.Q. said Crimshaw's guardian devil gave him the strength to*

ram the cart into Double's knee. ("Man, Satan's like that. You oughta know that from workin wit Crim!")

There was strange restless silence before Vole replied. "Is that what's scaring you to death? What have you got to lose?" She stopped for a while, then threw out in a rush as if dammed up too long with a gush of her feelings now at high tide: "You hold your *own* self back! Well you do! Look at Johnson and that senseless P.Q. They've still got their salaries, haven't they? Of course! With all their jive and who-shot-john, they've still got their salaries and they know enough to keep them! Both those niggers'll be shuckin and jivin all the way to the retirement office!"

With this last, I'm aghast; I've never heard Vole talk like this before—something's up here that's new and it's out of control—but wait, listen up, Double's speaking again—

"Look, I hate to say this, cuz it gives me brick-wall-itis even to *think* of runnin back through this again— But WHAT DID I SAY, Woman?! Didn't I say I'll think of somethin?"

"That was this afternoon," Vole cracked back, "a lifetime ago!"

Then, as Vole goes on to rant to herself ("THERE'S SUCH A THING AS TIME TO ACT!") I hear Double begin to speak clearly with vigor, though Vole seems not to hear or care to dig his monotribe, just pursues her own line of gripe as if she's alone while Double leans into his peeve with full speed, without need of her audience. . . .

"Got-DAMN, Woman! I'm used to standin on my own two feet! You think I'm lookin FORWARD to you bringin in the only bread an all that lip to go with it?"

Oh God, his speech problem, like mine to this day, it's genetic— Can't help but shoot back with his bent sense of humor of course; as he sees it, it's just the thing for encounters with the low-humored who're bent forever on Keeping It Down for all time, constipating the world. Double was Double in time of crisis, believed in being himself at all times and so refused to adjust his output to responses around him . . . said other folks' ideas could ooze in any direction they pleased, but they'd have to flow around him being him. And he was right on so many levels, simple human interaction levels, where our understanding is so tainted by relationship stain that love exchange disintegrates by force of erosion on so many ridiculous levels: money problems, dead romance, ad-hoc hearing and speech problems of lover-combatants— so many levels completely absurd and hidden from view til they're stacked like early morning pancakes, perverse.

Vole and Double would be having one of their verbal skirmishes that always meant a t.k.o. in Vole's favor—she'd jab below the belt with rapid one-two retorts while Double stood with guard down, letting himself be pummeled to pulp except to say *"Right! You're ALWAYS right!"* his cursory defense in an ongoing call-and-wicked-response bout forever in motion, blow-trading on with no regard for ringsiders like me. I'd be shrinking behind a closed door nearby, waiting like ten-year-old Job for their word tryst to escalate into siege warfare, waiting with bubbling visions of Vole and Double sickening finally of stunted word struggle, so falling on each other with tangible axes and hammers to hack to finis—My green psyche and neon fantasy exploded their struggle to a crashing violent final resolution time and time again, unlike these insufferable anti-climaxes. . . .

But this time Double charges out of their discord room and heads straight to the hi-fi *(where he's stashed his machete?)* as I'm watching undetected, bracing for action, since in my role of innocent bystander I expect to be fatally involved by circumstance. But Double's got method in his madness, it turns out, so by the time I step into the room behind him, he's just opened the record bin to pull out a razorless record album . . . and he's holding the record gingerly between his palms in order to read the label. . . . Now he's slipping it onto the turntable. . . .

Then all in a jiff there's a musical fitting finale to all our confusion—not a crash-boom! symphonic finale, but a jazz trickle from the heart into heart-thumping ad-infinitum. Of all twisted endings, before my very ears "My Funny Valentine" eases through Miles Davis' instrumental mute into the room around us, weaving liquid lines of reconciliation between Double and Vole, between me and Double and Vole, between man, woman, child, and bleak city, crazy country, road-to-hell world, well-meaning universe— A meeting of the minds of shooting stars slapping five through fluid tactical space looking on. Meanwhile Vole feels the summons and so is making her way to join Double and me and the three of us are standing motionless, time dies, and each of us is lit by need for radical redemption. We're just there, corny, shining at each other til Double blasts out, "All right, huddle time!" and we grab for each other and start to hug, all in a bunch.

Disaccord and Disintegration

Why grin and bear it through fight after fight? They spent most of the time hollering overseas at each other. . . .

You love her though, fool! said the voice in his head.

From the car seat beside, Vole turned to face him. ". . . Turn that jump music down, man! You want the new neighbors to think we're some jiving, jumping Negroes popped up from Franklin Street?"

This at the end of his foregone surrender. When would Vole learn to think before she jumped for the hype, first in line, early bird to a fault? What twisted impulse could drive any screwball to fishin around in whitefolks' minds in her spare time, when she wasn't on duty and it wasn't a case of survival? And not just fishin—Vole's a raggedy black miner, tongue hangin' out, pannin for foolsgold in 4/4/ time. . . .

Ok, I'll bite, Double thought. What *would* happen if worse comes to worse, and the new neighbors are blasted outa their Swing an their Dixieland? So they learn to stretch their jazz past the stand-in stage, that's all! An now for a quick plunge into the counter-offensive, cause that's what be-bop is—the threat of black music turnin back outsider-black, leavin white wallflowers all over the place, tryin to jive to a beat that blows their souls outa socket. So turn the sound up, not down. Cure us all. Take us as far off the level as you can get!

What you blackfolks need is a strong redeemer figure to lead you thru your blues.

Take a look at Fletch Henderson. One baby boy born black behind enemy lines, way down yonder in foreign turf Dixie. Born with nerve enough to be a musical genius. Sent to earth with madman potential. As a matter of course, this cat's story rolls right on downhill from there. Right on through the shortest distance between two black & white points, til his case lands smack in the middle of what you could call a ongoin border dispute of the mind. This is a story of internal strife. A folk tale.

Go to school and learn (to) trade: Vole and her dream.

Ask Fletch what his chemistry degree was worth while he was busy peddlin his musical charts to Benny Lootman for a petty piece-a chump change. Ole Fletch, invisible King of Swing, writin, arrangin an jammin for Lootman. Did everything but prop up Benny's clarinet. $37.50 per stunt is what Fletch had to show. Ask him did his chemistry degree teach him anything about *that* standard equation. Or about the chemical composition of a masked man, an his faithful native companion.

Hit it!

Luck bops in slumming, wearing a shiny red dress. Dragging a dirty handkerchief. Oobly blop; it hits the floor. (Don't yall jump at once, boys!) While over in the corner of her recent past lies a sorry soul with a death grip on his dreams.

"Well, there your folks were," Vole's telling Double by this time, with her taut tan face turned toward him, "up there with your president, threatening to kick off a mass march in Whitehouse City, right in the public eye. Well at least we got *Brown v. Board of Education* out of that one."

"Yeah, some more of jimcrow's tailfeathers," Double said to Vole. "Then it's double on back to the slums, y'all—hut-two. . . . Hold that Mason Dixon line!" He caught my eye in the rearview mirror and squeezed me a broad brash wink.

It was 1954, the year of our Move, to a brand new neighborhood with my strongest memory of black&white together, Integrated. We're first on the block to integrate—integrate, disintegrate, integrate; I integrate, you integrate, he, she, or it integrates; then we all disintegrate. . . . In-tee-grey-shun: strange word, weird vibe to me at the time, 'cause eight-year-olds're still connected to the earth and still take its cues. We had come to the block just to integrate, or so it seemed at the time due to everyone's feverish focus. Actually, we had simply come to that neighborhood in search of a choice bungalow built for three in an oasis of grass and trees, which is what we found, along with the surrounding bog of stagnant consciousness that bordered the house on all four sides.

"Forget the confusion though," Double told me in my consternation of adjustment to the neighborhood attitude toward our coming. "Never let yourself slide into being dependent on other folks' praise or blame, no matter who they are, or who they think they are."

"Besides, we're on our way up in the world," Vole threw in for weight. "And here in this part of town it's *up*, or medium-up at least, so that's why we're here!"

(Oh I get it, I thought. This is the tail end of Up, so we've hopped on its back and we're ready to ride to the end of the line.)

"Well we needed to move," Vole went on, "so how else could it be?" She was thinking of Dwen, a personal friend married to a doctor who was sharp as a whip and twice as rash. How when Dwen and her bitter half bought their new home in Saint Lou's suburban Chouteau Plateau, the neighborhood welcome wagon screeched onto the contract scene with a red-hot offer to buy their home-to-be out from under them *(Hell, you can make a profit, and please niggers, now just go away!)*—a pitiful pop-up from *Crazin' In The Sun*.

"Anyway," Double told me while looking at Vole, "the whites all around'll grow accustomed to us in due time, but we won't take low while they go about it. We won't act other than ourselves while they're knocking themselves out, acting like *them*."

("Well how do you like that?" said the scalawag who lived in my head. "This stuff's odd and you know it—stranger than fiction with riddles thrown in. You can tell it's the start of something real big with sharp teeth up ahead. So brace yourself for the bite soon to be!")

"See?" Vole said moments later to Double. "Even the child has a rudimentary grasp of what Integration means to her life." I had asked whether I'd be going to a new school now and if it would be a better one since the coming of Integration, a new magic word that I still was trying to decode, this time by way of an article that Vole's reading from a folded newspaper in her lap as we're riding in our questionable Studebaker with the first trip's worth of our family goods. My best things've been left behind as a matter of grown-up course, including precious, squeezy, one-eyed Scottie—I'll find this out in later trauma—he's small, black, and full of stuff just like me. But

"Just listen to this," Vole said suddenly, to Double's cursory glance and following shrug. "It might help you put on a new point of view.

" 'Yesterday will go down in history,' " she read, " 'as the day of the blockbusting Supreme Court decision in *Brown v. Board of Education*. . . .' " She stopped to laugh. "Integration busted our block, all right! Just watch. Now that we're here, the 'necks'll be moving out in droves." She paused to wave elaborate farewell to invisible bigots nearby. "*Bye!*" She stretched her jaws in a thin stingy smile. "And good riddance to *any* numbskull who's not ready for the boon of the future, In-tee-grey-*shun*. Yea, team!" She let out a chuckle.

"Just read the thing, willya?" Double said finally on top of Vole's spasm of laughter. Vole widened her eye-easy eyes to level a look aimed at Double. Then slowly she shot back with consummate cool. "That's just what I intend to do," she said as she picked up her paper and read. . . .

" 'An opinion handed down by Chief Justice Earl Warren unanimously overruled the separate-but-equal doctrine of *Plessy v. Ferguson*, and held that *de jure* segregation—"

"What's *'de jure'*?" I asked Vole in mid-stream of her reading.

"According to law," she said sharply.

"That's *'de facto,'* " said Double.

" *'De jure,'* " Vole said in her tone of don't-irritate-the-irritant—"*De jure*: according to law. *De-FACT-toe*: in fact. 'The court held that *de jure* " (here she stopped to look for a moment at Double's innocent profile; he's looking ahead now, straight at the road)" '. . . that *de jure* segregation in public schools was unconstitutional. The court stressed that *the badge of inferiority stamped on minority children by segregation hindered their full development'* " (Vole's emphasis) " 'no matter how equal the physical facilities.' " With this last, Vole slapped her newspaper shut and turned to smile oddly at me.

"So?" Double said to her side-angled back. "What's that got to do with us moving into this neighborhood an living in this community?"

Vole jerked to face front. "Don't you see?" she said with spare patience. "Now that the N-Double-A's got the ball in this case, it'll be a precedent for all *kinds* of public accommodations all over this land of the free!"

"So what? Even when we're accommodated in

public—we're still gonna be Negroes, won't we?"
Double throws this out with such seeming naiveté in
his casual boil-it-down way that I can't help but
laugh out loud in my backseat gallery post, making
for a combination of maddening cues which incensed
Vole to say, "What the hell's *that* supposed to mean?
This is what we've been fighting for, for lo these
many years! Full equality under the law! Wake up,
man!"

"The way I see it," Double says with his same easy
air, "the real reason the Negro hasn't been accepted is
. . . because he's a *Negro*!"

This brass tacks analysis causes Vole to lean back
in her seat with eyes closed and jaws tight, and I
can't resist, in nervous confusion I resort to my standard loud silly laugh. This particular fight of Double's and Vole's seems deadly intense yet harmless
somehow, maybe 'cause it's not personal . . . or is it?
But anyhow now's no time for me to muddle through
their fuss, I say to myself—my goal's to decipher this
Integration thing.

The car moves ahead slowly, and I note that Double's driving with extreme care as we pass row after
row of well-tended trees lining curbs of flat houses
with square boxed-in lawns. I can see now that this
neighborhood is what I took to be a park up ahead,
and I wonder with glee if we'll live here, in Dick and
Janeland, with green all around and stand-still whites
poised in every direction. They're staring at us like
we're on parade and that's good, I think; I feel like a
celebrity—like sensational Lena Horne to be exact, in
her triumph on parade at the end of World War II
when she came to Saint Lou to celebrate and sing

up a storm while bystanders stood by and adored her as she blew kisses from her color-full float passing through—Double's told me that story so many times. . . .

And hey, looka there, in front of that house with the grey stony front, there's a white man with a lawnmower—he's got no uniform on like the whites in the old neighborhood . . . Dig! His snow-white arms are hanging right out in public! I take the opportunity to wave. He stops, frowns, and mows the other way. Must didn't see me.

"You can climb every rung of the white man's ladder to success," Double's saying to Vole, "and you'll still get kicked in the teeth at the top. An no amounta education, 'good taste,' or milk-bathing will get the Negro into American society. Fact is, no amounta *any*thing will get you into the white man's world, until you turn white!"

"Oh, right," Vole said in feigned delight, brushing her hands together as well, that's that—a gesture that fails to serve notice to Double who doesn't even see it; his eyes are focused straight ahead.

"An you Negroes can *keep* lookin to kindly Uncle Integration to boost you through the ranks," Double says further, glancing over at Vole who's now had enough; forget this flanking defense, she'll have to put stock back in frontal attack.

"I want what's *mine* under the law!" Vole shot at Double.

"But that's just the problem," Double fired back. "It's only the *law*."

"What?"

"An the law is only a means to an end."

"Well, buddy," Vole said with a fed-up resolve, "I'm gonna take my means and use it to crack open every end I come across!" With her arms crossed in front of her chest, she wrenched to face the door at her side in the silence that crashed down around her.

When would he learn not to be held back? There was Daddy Hannibal, riverboating up and down the redneck Mississippi, waiting his tables so that all of us could go to college, a miracle of mashed-down pride and proud make-do, Mama Rose's no-end make-do— She's make many a meal from cast-off canned goods and never let blood to say never, just bled her turnips every day; she drained all the gall juice from never.

Then in came the sieve-sifting sound of Ethel Waters singing "Jazzin' Babies' Blues" with Fletch Henderson at sizzling keyboard behind her, cooking up a feast of sharps and flats since as Double said, "Black keys are the spice, and Fletch always cooks it spicy," (regardless of fate and foreclosed future, at least for an indigo interlude). Vole snapped to now with a start—Double had turned up his music again, the music he "hid in" to hear Vole, who'd tell it the way that she felt it, though Double of course saw it differently—two views at the scene of a love-clouded accident.

You had your low-life do-nothings on one hand, according to Double—if it wasn't for soon-to-be Saturday night, these were the jokers who wouldn't bother to get up in the morning; and on the other hand were your "books-or-bust ambassadors busy tryin to book up on equality so they can sneak up and tap it on the tail in the dark. Now these characters are always ready to downrate the past at the drop of a cap. To them, "slave" is a dirty word, like the blues, a bad image. . . .

Did I hear you say 'the blues'? Man, don't you know these new-negroes ain't got time for nothin that brings to mind no moanin an groanin. Man oh man! But who'm I tellin? You know it too that once you get started, it's the devil, if you want to put it that way, bein able to stop. Don't let these new-negroes get started! Man, the blues to these chumps is a hell-drove springboard to the land of cotton. Presto! Spring back to dose old nightmare stockincap days back in the land of the gladly forgotten!

Flying Black Aces and Bound-to-Ground Spades

"In MY kosmos," said the Kat,
"there will be no feeva of discord!"

Double read this Krazy Kat comic at a time when it was his habit to fill in the blanks of my primary school lessons with whatever noteworthy tips that would put me in the know. It's that fever of discord, he said, that causes all our constant scuffling in wild directions while we scramble over our fellow fools, stomping their dreams as we go. Matter of fact, Double said, damn near all our deviling of each other can be traced to mankind's original crab-in-the-barrel attitude. (As soon as a crab starts to inch his way to the

34

mouth of the barrel, another crab reaches up and snatches him back down.)

"See," he went on, "some of the human race are dispatched to earth as dream-busters. An they take their charge serious as all get-out, workin like they're on commission at a hundred G's per pop!" Which is why, when it came to guarding my dreams still shiny and green, Double would act first and think later— something just snapped in him and steered him to seek out and destroy the danger. Like that time I was eight years old and had wandered across the grocery store, beating my gums with passersby til I encountered one old redneck who didn't mind stooping to bedevil an open-faced kid.

"Well damn these plums an thangs," he'd begun through a side-tilted grin, "I'd rather have a sweet lil cullud gal lak yew. Pity you ain' ripe yet, but ah bet yore mighty jewcee. . . ." He was busy whispering to me, churning out his scheme of the moment when all of a sudden I look up and here comes past-tense peaceable Double barrelling down the row behind the cracker's back, Double's big bright eyes nearly twice their usual size, moustache-looking eyebrows hunched downhill and riding the bridge of his nose, blunt nose flaring at the nostrils, skin color gone from milk-chocolate brown to the tone of blood mixed with mud, shoulders hunched so it looked like he was back in his zoot suit, fumes all around him that seemed visible and incandescent, made him look like twice his five-foot-ten and wham! Mr. Nasty never knew what hit him til he hit the ground. Musta thought it was the lightning wrath of the Lord, which it was in a way, as Double grabbed for my hand and we made for the door of outside salvation.

Double dug his dreams and mine too as his young chip—was religious about em the way some folks believe in straight here-and-now life. "Your dreams are your parachute," Double would say. "Let some joker fool aroun an cut your safety string, then when you need to bail out, which is damn near all the time in this life, just see how you freefall and land!"

How you land, how you stand, how you balk at command—"As for sleep-dreams," Double went on to say, "it's lucky they bear resemblance to waking world life, as twisted and warped as it is. That's what they're for: dreams are to help you unscramble the maze of your life, if you got sense enough to follow their lead."

Double said he'd been thinking in his sleep about the foodstore fight and our consequent flight, when suddenly an army convoy appeared as Act Two. . . .

The convoy passed once, Double said, and I was standing next to him at the time, his nine-year-old sidekick. When the bivouac passed slowly the first time, he hesitated to point it out to me he said, because somehow he knew it'd be coming back, could feel it in his regular sign-seeing way, he said, knew it like the black of his hand (his words and he laughed). Then he grew serious, 'cause he knew he had to tell me about the bivouac's return. . . .

When the convoy came back, Double said, tanks went tearing through town at full speed, charging foot soldiers among its own troops, including one man who was carrying a young woman piggyback along with a small child who was clinging to the side of the woman, all sprawled out in a heck of a shaky position. Then a bullet-nosed army bus came ramming through it all. The bus was that nasty khaki color—"the color of grief sent to bring back relief"—and at its wheel was an American airman with a red-faced grin and icy eyes who put him in mind of the Yankee paratroopers, *Fallschurmjäger*, who'd nightmared his dreams since the days of his doubleedged combat duty in World War II in Germany.

There were days in Kurfürstendamm when Double saw to it that he was never alone, days following his recent unwelcome by military men on the bitter side of the War Department's new color-mix tactical act.

"You can take a cracker out of the boondocks," Double said then to Lester at his side, "take him out of the boondocks, push him through OCS, an set him up overseas in a salt-n-pepper platoon, the world's Eighth Wonder of the pal-in-misery principle, History on Parade, opportunity of a lifetime, an what've you got? A redneck cracker with delusions of plantation kicks."

"Or kinks," said Lester. "An you can kick til you're blue in the face. Now take a peckerwood—"

"Thinly disguised in GI fatigues," Double drawled, "—your Stepuncle Sam's world-famous fatigues. . . . By the way, all *my* fatigues are on the inside of my skin, jack."

"In our soul, man."

"Now you're cookin," said Double. "An don't forget, there's a million more screwball ofays to come, 'round about midnight to be precise, with their brickbats an bottles in hand, just to break you in to their frame-a mind about your threat to the life of their main man, Jim Crow."

"Call it Basic Trainin!"

"You said it, pal."

Those were days of forked loyalty, or war within war. It had been a scant two weeks before his arrival in the Allies-captured town of Kurfürstendamm that Double was assigned with black troops deployed to destroy an enemy tanker off the coast of Germany—a waypaving feat that was noted in newspaper features like:

BLACK REDTAIL ANGELS STRIKE AGAIN WITH SUCCESS

Kurfürstendamm, Jan. 23, 1943— *"They flew right out of the night!" Daring and determined, feared fighter pilots of the Nazi-dubbed "Schwartze Vogelmenschen" [Black Birdmen] staged yet another successful strafing mission in the Gulf of the Rhine resulting in the first sinking of an enemy destroyer with close-range gunfire. Flying P–51 type aircraft with identifying red paint on their tail assemblies, the aerial gunners are members of one of the four squadrons designated as the 332nd Fighter Group in the "Noble Experiment" under command of Negro Colonel Benjamin O. Davis, Jr. To date the 332nd Fighter Group is credited with being the sole unit not to lose a single bomber to enemy fighters in 195 bombing missions over strategic targets in Europe.*

"These guys have a lot of heart," said General Eisenhower, who was impressed by the operation. "Whatever your feelings on race, you've got to take off your hat to these boys. They're true blue Yanks who hate the mere sight of a Nazi."

But Nazis were demons with little regard for geography; the Allies were cursed with near-Nazis too as was proven one night by the *Fallschurmjäger* he'd never forget, three hellbent American airmen in hooded dennison smocks who prowled their post's new colored barracks, their faces lit white by the light of the moon. . . .

"Ovah heah," the wraith-thin lieutenant whispered to the two men stumbling through bushes behind him.

"*Where?*" said a voice of rattled shrapnel. A thickset trooper stepped forward. He stared at his older companion in the dimness.

"*Lookit,*" the taller corpsman insisted, pointing toward a dark form barely visible in the mist up ahead.

"Well lookie, lookie," the younger paratrooper said in a stop-dead tone of voice. The man was short and squat, his mouth rimmed with a grim grizzle of hair. "Whut have we heah?" He stooped to squint again at Double who's partly hidden now by an outbranch of bushes beyond as he voids nature's course in a stream of the Rhine.

"Who goes there?" Double jerked up warily, one hand near the leg of his jumpsuit though he sees nothing yet, just feels presence by reflex, it's nature, til the first *Fallschurmjäger* steps into the moonlight.

"What yall want?" Double stayed still.

"Nevah min' the querstions, boy," said the loose rattling voice. The lanky trooper appeared with the stocky man and a third airman bringing up his rear.

"Yeah, *we'll* do the quizzin, nigger," the lanky airman said.

"Yuh ain' got the raht sperit, boy." The thickset trooper grinned at Double. "What you apes go' celebrate when the war's over, an you heroes finely git whut's comin to yuh, huh?"

"Yeah!" said the eager first soldier. "They never shoulda had a coon unit fightin a white man's war in the first place!"

"They say they won't the war ta be a lessin for the world—thass whut they *say*, anyhow. . . ." The third man spoke quietly, as if to himself. He looked past Double toward the bushes ahead, then turned to glance back for a moment that seemed to contract in the chilly night air.

"Aw, you know niggers cain' stick when the goin gits rough!" the second airman said. He looked intently at the third airman heedless beside him.

" *'Cose* they cain' stick!" The tall paratrooper lumbered toward Double. "Whatcha got to say to *that*, dinge?"

Double tucked one hand in the sleeve of his dennison smock. From somewhere in nearby black barracks came a gut-deep laugh that echoed in hollow stillness where he stood.

"Speak up, coon." The squat man spat in the mud. "Niggers cain' even talk."

For an instant the lanky soldier's skin darkened and faded from view. A fine prickling mist had begun to fall. "Whatdja *expeck* in a coon?" His face went dead with causticity. " 'Ain' nuthin wrong wid America that Hitler kin fix!' that nigger colonel said. Didja heah 'im? Talk lak he own the store!"

"Got nerve of a monkey an then some. Did ah heah 'im?" The anxious man choked on the words. "When ah heered 'im say that, ah thoed mah shawt wave down an it lak ta bus' inter a hunnert pieces!" The shorter airman aimed his gaze at Double. "I *hate* a loud mouf coon. This country don' need no jig ta speak fuh us."

"Waal, we *got* one!"

Double turned his eyes toward the tall soldier who spoke with disgust.

The stocky airman spoke. "All we need in this war is a jigaboo mouthpiece!" He stared at the third trooper for a moment suspended in time. "Yew was there too," he said to the third man finally. "Yew heard the nervy nigger on the shawt wave jes' lak we did."

The third man declined to speak.

"Somebody needs ta put a end ta that nigger sass," the high-strung trooper said.

Needles of moisture warmed and then chilled Double's skin. He heard himself speak. "You ain' lookin for me. I just came out here to take a leak an I—"

"Yew tellin us whut we lookin fer, boy?" the quick trooper grinned.

Double stepped back into sod like slush beneath the heals of his boots. "I'm just sayin yall don't want *me*."

The first man spoke softly, with clattery calm. "Yew ain' tallin *us* nothin, coon." He smiled to himself.

Instantly the heavy man spoke. "Mebbe yuh don' lak livin!"

"I tell you, I just got to barracks," Double said. His next words seemed to push their way out. "An I ain't plannin on going no place else."

"Gittin sassy?"

Double could smell the rankness of the rangy soldier's breath in the moist night air.

"Yew heah the cheek-a this nigger?" The tall trooper turned to the speechless third man at his rear. "See how he is? He needs somebody ta teach 'im howta *ack*."

41

"Hey, lem*me* learn 'im!" the squat soldier said.

"Wait jesta minute," the gangly man said with a grin. "Lemme talk ta the nigger." He paused for a moment, looking at Double. "Say nigger," he said directly to Double. "Did yuh see how the watt men fought brave in the air war, an the niggers, yer sneakin squad number three-three-two, they got coal feet an hadta radio back to base for the watt men's go ahead?"

"They didn't know *what* the fuck ta do!" said man number two. " 'Flyin Nigger Aces' mah butt! Ah cawl em the Flyin Nigger Spades!" Hoots ricocheted in the rain. "Whut yuh got to say ta that?"

"The Flyin Nigger Spades ain' shit on a tooth-pick!" the thin man insisted. "Whut yuh say ta *that*, dinge? Huh?"

When the man prodded him heavily, Double felt flesh in his inner jaw give and grow slack. "Speak up, nigger," the loud mouthed soldier said. "We cain' heah yuh!"

For an instant Double's mind shifted from over-drive to low gear: *The Flying Black Aces were just ordinary spades.* . . . He swallowed and spoke with words like stones in the sling of his cheek. "I don't know nothin 'bout no scam. All I know's we lost 66 men an we got 32 shot-down p.o.w.'s—"

The thin trooper cocked his head to one side. "Don't git smart now, boy," he said.

"That ain' the end of it!" the stocky man said with stiff glee. He circled Double with anticipation. "Don't-chew forgit, yew talkin t'*white* men, nigger," he said through a vise of his teeth.

In silent slow motion, the third man shrugged and turned to look behind him. "Less go," he said finally.

"Jes' leave the jig be." He seemed to be listening for a sound yet unheard. "It ain' worth the sweat," he said in the still acrid air. "I ain' studdin whut he thinks."

There was only the sound of boot-splintered bone as Double sank to his back in the mud. The hot-headed airman leaned back and aimed a second kick at Double's groin. "Yew still sassy, dinge?" he said to the fallen form near his foot.

"Put 'im straight!" The stocky paratrooper shuffled from one cochrane boot to the other.

"Hold on!" The third man's voice was far-off and low, the disjointed voice of a dream.

"Where's mah stiletto?" the rusty voice said.

"Use yer commando!" the eager voice urged.

As Double lay still, something happened quickly: There was noise of a scuffle and a pommel-heavy knife submerged in the mire next to Double's prone body.

"Hey, cut it out!" the squat soldier spat at the third with surprise. "Whut yew turnin' into? A pissin jig protector?"

"Yew gittin yella or whut?" The tall trooper advanced toward the quieter man.

"Aw, jes' leave 'im be!" the quiet man said, turning to leave. "Ah'm in this war, I gotta be heah—I ain' got no say far's that goes. But lef' up to me, Ah ain' got no fight wit no critter walks upright. Ah'll stand on mah word about that!"

The Run-Down at Ringside

To know just what happened to Double in life, you'd have to know Double and his talent for strikin out on his own, all alone, no matter what the stakes or situation, like a crazy niggah from outa this world and beyond its borders all over the place!

Now don't get me wrong. My man never tried to go for bad, though Double could *kick tail* when necessity struck—I oughta know; see, I can hold my own in a lil lightweight prize fight myself, ringside or sidewalk!

Like I say though, Double, he'd never use his dukes for the hell of it, cuz he wud'nt studdin no show of any type; didn't go for stylin and profilin, which was strange in a young blood from the sticks in '38 . . . tho he was known for jivin the chicks into giving him some trim—more than his share, I might add.

44

"*What you doin?*" *I used to ax 'im. "Tryin to run thew all the leg there is?*"

Yet somehow, due to force of his hoo-doo, none-a the frails got bitter about it, it didn't seem to faze em none; not one-a the skirts seemed to feel a thing but the urge to get next to the cat for more of the same seven & six!

Yeah, Double, he did dig the chicks, but he didn't hold no truck wit monkeyin aroun for the hell of it—had better things to do, he said, and no time to waste. So we was never runnin buddies—Double never was a cat for runnin the street; never even used to hang aroun what he called the "fool hall"—though he did used to haunt Zoot's barbershop, "headquarters" he called it back then.

The "big view" of things is what Double took, accordin to himself. "It stands to reason some folks might won't be able to figure me out," he said once. "And that's solid! It gives me more room for me to be me, while I do what I came here to do!"

Well now. The "big view"! Fact is, if there was anything in it at all, whatever the problem or cause of confusion, Double's the one who'd pick up on it, and how! From the moment he hit town, it was clear to us all that now here was a cat fulla double-edged steel who would call his own shots in a zone all his own!

That's PQ's view of what made Double Double, and what brought his later dead-ended life trouble— Yet, when I think of Double I can see him now, tall and red-brown skinned with big bright eyes and wide open smile, his hair woolen soft and naturally peaked and valleyed by his fingers in defiance of the artful washboard waves of his peers. He'd be standing centerstage in the barbershop, vocaleesing like no

45

tomorrow to the tune of "Flyin' Home" or a jam by one of the other bopcats, say Bird—*Ool ya koo, ah ruby do flew*—He'd wing his way through "Embraceable You," touch down for an instant, then turn into his dream of himself as cool smoothie bassman plucking fast clean bass— whoompwhoompwhoompwhoomp, eight beats to a line. (*Walk* it!) He'd bop right up the bridge of the tune and whop, double stop, whop dop didee—he'd choke the time then let it breathe with me jiving to the beat right beside him: "Walk it, Daddy!"

"Atta baby!" Double'd say to rusty-kneed me. "And if *that* don't git it—"

"Don't be so *mean*!" PQ would shout.

"*Live* a little!" Zoot threw out.

In this way Double'd school me each day *re* the skills of our outstanding stalwarts, starting with our musicmakers who managed to transmute hard times into good—something he'd do yet himself, he said, though he'd let himself get waylaid away from his goal. Then he'd extol the force of our athletes, empowered by faith and sheer stick-to-it stamina regardless of setbacks and getbacks they stumbled upon. He showed me these things, Double said, in order to teach me to see the invisible rules that allowed just these few of our forerunners to waypave their own path in America—to till in the potholes the whites left behind.

To sprint beyond the hold-back blocks— The issue's intact through the years of time's roll from the moment of Double's debut in Saint Lou when still green with his seventeen years of backwoods background, the lure of Saint Lou being boil-downable to his aim to go to school here in the land of educational promise—to Harriet Beecher Stowe Teachers College to be precise, Stowe being the dream and necessity all wrapped up in one. There's H. B. Stowe College for The Colored where men including Double and cronies are passed to the second rung of the four-year stint, cutoff point for males being second year junior-college level, while women are processed for four years toward school teaching over and out and up above heads of husbands-to-be who're spun off in a dozen different unskilled directions, Stowe or no Stowe. School days are just a gesture for Double and his pals unless they have long bread wherewithal to make it to further education far away from home semi-sweet home. Yet he'd heard of a black man who'd patented so many inventions that his name came to fame in common conversation. *(Is it the real McCoy?)* In those days, Double said, he didn't rule out the possibility of an invention of his own on the scale of McCoy's automatic lubrication device that revamped the factories, so he started his habit of note-taking then, by listing the names of black inventors of standard conveniences conveniently overlooked—the cotton gin, traffic light, air brake, gas mask, electric third rail, machine-made shoes, you name it!

So that I'd be able to see and i.d. with the history before me— "To open up your window on the world," Double said then to me at his knee—he'd tell of his exploits and life explorations. ("If all you can see is borders and blurs close at hand, then don't wait for your cue; it's all up to you to extend your own vision—to focus on finish lines way up ahead, far beyond what's already in view!")

It was in light of this insight that Double told me of his first arrival in Saint Lou at downtown Union Station with its noisy lifelong fever of trains of escape. On the morning he came here he said, rugged ice was beheading trees in a step-by-step pattern, slicing the Woezarks into piles of white chips and sucking the winter Mississippi River into liquid points like dingy frozen custard. It was that same relentless frost that filled the brick courtyard surrounding the station, milk white sleet blanketing statue-fountains of anatomical men with muscles frozen in arrested action, their mouths spitting streams of frozen dreams under overcast hopeful sky of 1938. This was the year of Double's first coming to Zoot's barbershop in the Ville by the side of the tracks, where PQ presided by reading the news of the day in his own indomitable do-or-die way. . . .

STREET DANCE IN SAINT LOUIE
NEGROES IN GAY CELEBRATION OF
JOE LOUIS'S TRIUMPH

(That's how it was, Double said later in recap to me; the post-fight streets were full of black ecstatics—born again believers washed in holy drench redemption from jobless-relentless-grubless blues, saved by the way from their barbwire day-to-day.)

Saint Louis, June 23, 1938—Saint Louis' Negro section, with a population of 232,000, staged a gay celebration of Joe Louis's one-round victory over Max Schmelling last night. Shots were fired in the air, firecrackers set off, trolley poles jerked from street cars and some windows broken.

Crowds poured into the streets a few moments after Schmelling's defeat was broadcast from Chicago. Dancing Ne-

*groes covered the pavements and tied up traffic. Nightclubs in
the district reported the liveliest business since New Year's Eve.*

"Cholly can tell us all about that," a lean dark cat
named Lester threw out.

"Thass right, put me on the spot," Cholly said.
"Make like you wasn't there too."

Lester raised his eyes in fake surprise. "Man, I'm
just tryin to give you credit. Hell, you was the chief
of the party, an I was just an ordinary Indian."

Cholly fell out. "Didn't we ride it high?"

The rest of the regs were slapping skin when PQ
cut in. "Wait. Listen at this." Then he read:

*BROWN BOMBER KAY-OES NAZI-GERM
IN ONE-HALF ROUND ONE*
"When I got in the ring with Schmelling that second time,"
*Joe Louis said, "I was in there for a lot more than money.
There's nothing wrong with America that Hitler can fix!"*

"Over and out!" came somebody's shout, sparking
a yowl of accord among barbershop brethren. Among
them was Les with his side-parted conkoleen shiny
and patent—leatherish, a brown unkinked cap that he
wore as a crown—Lester who feigned a fall whenever
he laughed as if he was knocked off his feet, bent into
pretzel shape now next to no-jive, stay-alive hard-
jobbing Zoot in the stern of the mayhem today and
always. ("You bet your life!") Over in the corner near
Arvis, Aldrich and the rest of the crew was fast-
talking cool-walking Cholly holding forth from his
usual throne of engagement, an empty customer's
chair at his station, the heed-lacking feedback seat of

the scene ("Sez who? Sez *you*. Well gee, mah knee!").
And next to the coatrack was bearded black Mack,
barbershop elder, who'd served in World War I at the
front and lived to tell it and tell it and tell it some
more. . . .

PQ spoke out above the din with his freckle-faced
grin. "All I'm sayin is, if Joe Louis hadn't been a
colored cat, all these bitter jokers'd be goin wild with
glee right now. 'America won the fight of the world,'
they'd be sayin. 'Our American man on American
land, while Europe's at war overseas,' so they'd say."

"Damn right," Cholly said. "Now ain't that a blip?"

Like discrimination between night and day, or spontane-
ous blitz of black on white for a change. (Time, pappa!)
Two minutes for Joe Louis to turn him (Hitler/Goebbels/
Schmelling) every way but loose. Then, Wham! White
Hope's on his back.

"Hey, Hope!" growled grizzled Maclean in his thick
whiskey voice. *"Sprechen zie schwarz blitzkrieg?"*

"Say what?" Zoot shot back.

Like a bolt from the black came Mack's answer.
"Uh, do you speak black lightning war?"

PQ stopped on a dime to look over at Mack in
mock horror, then read straight ahead with a while
side-bent smile.

SCHMELLING'S DEFEAT VIEWED AS "BAD LUCK"

PQ covered his head from the roar of resistance
that rose in the way that the sun rose and set. Over a
jangle of jeers— *"Now that's a neat switch." "Ain't that*
a scream?"— PQ shouted the follow-up news with
thick gusto. ("I'll force feed you fellas if need be!")

BE-BOP, RE-BOP

Kurfürstendamm, June 23, 1938—Kurfürstendamm's reaction to Joe Louis's knockout victory over Max Schmelling in two minutes four seconds was one of almost unbelieving astonishment.

The opinion generally expressed was that Schmelling had had the bad luck at the very beginning of the fight to step into a terrific left. . . .

"His 'luck' was off, jack," PQ said to the throng with a thin impish grin, just as Double stepped up to join in. "From the moment he laid eyes on Joe!"

"From the minute Joe dusted him off!"

"Decked 'im, you mean."

"Wham! Wham! Wham! Here's how Joe whaled 'im."

"Aw, cut the corn. Joe made Max lose his good ways."

"Don't kid me like that—"

"I kid you not."

"Them Nazis like Schmelling ain' got no good ways. Stompin a Jew or a Spade however they can, that's they favorite pastime!"

"Aw, Pappa Stoppa, don't be stiff. We all got our pastimes! Now what's wrong with that?"

"Man, you a *mess.*"

Double bent to his worn duffle bag and took out a small spiral notebook he'd felt pressured to buy without knowing why, eyed it a second, then wrote with a short stubby nub of a pencil, *"Colored champions in history! Stowe Teachers College! Nothing can stop me!"* He stuffed the notebook handy in his back pocket, thinking of his pull from the nightridden farm in the Texas Panhandle to this wildcard future here in brightlights Saint Lou.

But Nat King Cole's RCA Victorized voice was filtering into the room right that instant in an untamed scat-happy croon. . . . *"I don't want fish cakes and rye bread, you heard what I said—tomahtoes hurt my pride! I want the flim-flam sauce with the awesome fakes . . . and shoo-fa-fa on the side!"*

Double jumped up with evangelist's spirit, as if he'd been called by a weird roguish voice. With eyes snapped in a squint he plucked his make-believe bass in time to the tune, just as PQ eased into his view.

"Hey, nappy cap," said the rhiney-skinned man in a look-at-me loud-speaking voice. "Looks like all you need is some wood and some strings to bring this baby to life!" He reached out to grab Double's fantasy bass.

Zoot etched a thin razor line in a customer's pomade-waved head and laid down his shears. He bent a brash wink in the newcomer's direction and aimed his remarks straight to Les. "Get a loada that cat. It just shows to go, you can't judge a cat by his country-time rags. The dude may not be dry behind the ears, but he's no rinky-dink, I'm here to tell you. Watch him run it down."

Then's when Double spoke out in his sand-sifting way. "Well the way that I see it, a man's gotta make him some music by *some* kinda means. The first thing he needs is the druthers to want it. The next thing he needs is the gumption to work it, no matter who funs him or shuns him."

Lester went limp with a loose gimpy laugh. "No doubt about it, he set you PQ!"

"Yow!" PQ howled, but he wouldn't be done out

of his spotlight—he'd shine yet and still, so he snatched
up his news-sheet, proceeding to read:

HITLER, GOEBBELS SEND TOKENS TO CONSOLE
SCHMELLING'S WIFE
    "It's terrible that punches like that are permitted," said
blonde Miss Ondra of the blow that injured Max. "I didn't
know that they were allowed."

"Now just get to that." PQ beamed at Double.
Double shot back. "You said it. And *how!*"

II

Muz and the Sphere of Memory

Muz and the Sphere of Memory

Why is it that radical reviews always start at the core of your current and clack back through your mucked-up life? It's standard operating procedure; no one escapes the railroad express with its scenic view of the past.

In this way, in the liquor store of today, I find myself suddenly subjected to passing-flash memory of still-married me, sorrowful and contrite for being boozed again, and in front of husband Charlie, motherly Muz, and young chick Mia who's four years old at the time. This all goes down when it's 98-degree serious summer in Saint Brew and I've been tucked away all day with my usual beers on the back porch so that Mia can play outside where there's hope of a breeze. All day long I've been home, and I'm not the only one—we're all here, inside neighborly fences with our foodstamp beer and watermelons—students, artists, retirees, unemployees, and captive mothers like me, spontaneously combustible fire-tempered folks as far as the eye can see.

Before the day can broil away, I've wound up screaming fed-uply at Muz, which releases the regular rash of guilt and reproach from within, then I yank baby Mia and scream at her til she cries, due to fury at Muz and at Charlie who's squalled into his Me-Tarzan-You-Shit act; and hell, I'd rather be Cheetah than Jane—Cheetah's *supposed* to be slow so can excuse his shortcomings in matters of scuffling to please and then shuffling aside with a monkeyish grin. Charlie's been waving his paycheck in my face and enlightening me with wisdom like "I'm sick of your constant comments. Don't let your mouth take you where your ass can't follow!" which brings on my tailormaid trip of repentance for harmony's sake, so I smile and refuel with my beer after beer. . . . That's me for example, cooking subthermal Charlie a midnight supper when he gets in from the later day's work. And yep, that's the Kid again hovering over the stove, hand-slaving a poundcake solely for Muz. Hostility grates me like a gristmill, and I know what I'm doing yet do it anyway, nevertheless, asinine-regardless . . . stupid, stupid, Jane afterall.

My atonement includes mopping and scrubbing the kitchen and bathroom floors, all after a clandestine slap from Charlie back in the kitchen but I deserve it! I think at the time, and Charlie only hit me once—he held his temper this time, despite the lure of my guilt.

Why is it that I wash my sins away with repentant floor cleaner suds and a beer or two, feel confessional fresh, then am At It again in no time at all? I despise myself when I can't help but drink—I hate what I feel and hate what I do when my shadow splits off and takes over the show while I watch it from shut-away closeted wings, I see it upstage the bright best of myself. . . . Damn you, dense shade of relentless intent, bent on venting self-consummate force at any event, whenever my pressure cooks up to max— Hooch never helps and I know it!

Like this I go on thinking, chew-thought ruminating about past repeated error of the same foolish type, til deliberately as part of my cure from the lure of further gloomination, I conjure up the virulent vision of my healing throes after that booze bout of yore. Instantly I see Charlie, who lopes into view right on cue with his knack for kicking a sucker. I can still see him now, can't forget how, how he— See? He's dragging baby Mia into the bathroom to watch me throw up bile and drops of blood, my bitter dues on the installment plan once an hour, despite my dose of Pepto Dismal. . . .

Look! Look! See Mommy squirm!

So it is that noxious recall spews me into a course of the current and heaves me up to right now, where I am in this liquor store buying visiting houseguest Muz her fifth of Cutty Shark—this being my goal and sole mission. *Just show Muz how cope-able I am, now that I've moved on my own to San Fran. . . .* From here at the counter I can see the beer glistening in the back-of-store refrigerator, which I soon find myself headed toward in a natural way like the rest of recidi-vist nature. So what? So I'll pick up some cans of malt liquor. This stuff serves its purpose—it cures tough congestion, shrinks swollen membrains. . . . Ask the two women in line to the counter. Just to hear these she-roes talk, you know that they know what they're here for.

Woman One: ". . . *too* cold!"

Woman Two: "Was I cold? I said to George, 'Lis-ten. Our relationship, if you want to call it that, well it didn't exactly start out to be one of those everlastin hook-ups. I mean it had to end sometime, right? And now time's just up, that's all, no blame. . . . Had to bust myself right there; I almost said 'the jig'—'the jig is up.' Yeah, fool, the jig, the stroll, the hustle, and so's your slow drag through my life—"

"I hear you!"

"By the time we broke up, George was sayin 'Well wait. Let's talk, baby. Don't be rash.' "

"Say what?"

"Now you know I been tryin to talk to this nut for four years—"

"That all?"

"And by the time he hauls his wide-ego self over to tryin to get me back—when he finely drags his bag all the way over to the 'let's talk' stage, well it turns out we've developed these two different accents—not whole separate lingos, but damn close, worse even when you think about it. You're talkin the same, *sounds* almost the same, and that's what leads you off and runnin, see— But everything you say, you get 'Hello? Hello?' See what I'm sayin?"

"For sure."

"So all I want to know is, How come, when a man and a woman hook up in all seriousness and respect—this ain't no drop-in love affair now; no kid on the way or any other timebomb in the scene, just a matter of choice, adult agreement between two consenting fools— Why is it that from the moment you get married, the countdown to hell begins? Five, four, three, two. . . . *And now my friends, at the sound of the bang, your bag will turn into a box.* Hell, what's missing in this picture?"

A piece of familial puzzle—Muz has her own, which she brandishes the minute I'm back in the car. "For your sake," she says, "I hope Mia has a smooth adolescence! I know she's only nine now," she answers my quizzical eyebrows and forges ahead, "and I know you think there's a huge gap between mothering a child of nine and mothering a teenager-to-be. But believe me, adolescence is right around the corner. It'll be up on you before you know it!"

When I see her shoulders sag for a moment I can't help but remember how she turned to me with tears in her eyes at daybreak on the day after Double died at the axis of my adolescence, right when a Girl Needs A Father Most. "You're all I've got," Muz said at the time. And yet so far as a teenager, she said, I've been spending damn near all my better energy, working overtime at it, just grieving her to the hilt ("Words aren't made for this," she grieved), with my persistent Courting of Disaster. Then came the nostalgic tidbits from my mottled past, proof of my rotten response to the challenge of growing up, episodes handpicked and promptly produced, fresh from her timetight bag of miserable memories.

Now, as she turns to glance across the carseat at me, for a moment I look straight into the opaque wool brown of Muz' eyes and I'm struck by their lack of a spark of zest (as Double's had), and the old Eyeball Theory as Double called it comes ogling up from my childhood straight through my grownup cool.

According to Double's hypothesis, which dealt with eyes as windows of the soul, sole windows that the inner self looks through and can be seen in, one of the key signs when reading eyes is the presence or absence of telltale spark in the optical lens, that little flame flaring from time to time. Since Double's research had unearthed bright-eyed folks who were *bon vivants* and who yet were sparkless, his conclusion was the eyespark is produced by zest for life, but not vice-versa, in those who're on the up and up. So seeing lusterless Muz of today, I'm pierced from inside by a pang of connection with her ongoing grief and with her loss of hope in deadening widowhood. After all, I'm a widow too; look at my funereal marriage here on the bier.

"You know what though?" Muz said to me a scant year ago. "I keep thinking if I'd just gotten up there (to K.C. MO where Double'd moved in search of work)—if I'd've managed to go see him before he died, he never would've died. I know he wasn't *doing* for himself like he should've you know, and if I'd only made myself go on up there! But that was around the time the windows needed sealing remember? and everything all over the house would've got ruined, it was raining and storming all that winter, remember? But somehow I could have managed it; I should've done what my better judgment told me, should've followed my first mind, something *told* me—"

"Wait," I cut in, "hear me out. And I want you to know, if I seem like I'm not responding when you tell me something like this it's not 'cause I don't feel a thing or nothing, it's just that I try not to flap right off the top see. My way is to shut down and gather my steam for as long as I can; I just shut down all operations til I can hear myself think—"

"*Lord*, you're my daughter!"

"—so I can stop and mesh things through—"

"—just *like* me!"

"Now here's what I want to say—"

"You do exactly like me, that's me all over again!"

"All right now, let me express myself—"

"Ok."

"The thing to keep in mind is *we* don't say when it's time to die—"

"God says that; it's up to Him."

"We're not the ones who say when it's time to go; we can't postpone anybody's death when it's time for them to go. When it's time for them to go, then it's *time*—and they go."

"I'll buy that! Go on, you're *helping* me."

"Then too, his life had been painful for a long time now. We can't exactly peep the Spirit's hand you know, but sometimes I think *I* can tell what's on Her mind—"

"Now you're talking."

"So it was time for him to go. Besides, Double's still here you know. People don't evaporate when they pass, they literally pass into another phase just like everything else on this earth. The waves are the same waves, this is the same dirt we're walking—we keep digging up old shit from millenniums ago, don't we? And *we're* the same, same bodies even. God don't throw nothin away—"

"Go on; I'm with you—"

"Everything on this earth is recycled. And the world runs on a master plan down to the protoplasm. So are human beings the only exception? Aw, come on."

"Damn! You're helping me; you're good!"

"Coulda told you that."

"Oh you wouldn't be telling *me* anything. One thing about me, I'm wide awake in this world. Not too much slick stuff slides past me!"

Muz is silent now; she's facing the scene at the car window on her right, the outside world with its current view of the Spansamerica Pyramid glimmering in the heart of San Fran's Financial District for a concrete case in point, with its bustling office workers visible in fluorescent windows on their way to the downward escalator and out the front door. At the downstairs door they'll meet—I can see this upcoming incident and so feel like God for a moment—at the outer building door they'll meet a waiting bevy of slow-moving downhearted derelickeds gathered at the end of their own long hard hustle. These bums have dealt with flat-pocketbook office workers all day long, and hope hangs heavy in an empty hat outstretched by necessity. Two ragged men limp among the fleeing nine-to-fivers, begging-handout-denizens maintaining their own practical plodding pace in a whirlwind of commuters all around; but no one sees them, of course not—who'll look at those barely mobile mirrors of our desperation, inner wound in outer form?

Here on the edge of rush hour we're barely making any time at all up this hill of Sacramento Street, inching uphill toward gilded bliss of Nob Hill up ahead where the Mark Hopkins Hotel leans discreetly into view on the left and St. Mary's Cathedral is a squinted vision of faithful landmark up ahead on the right. Looking beside me at Muz' back, I can see her straightening erect in the airport last night saying, "Let me know when you see that Dowager's Hump again. . . ."

Dowager's Hump? I'd told her only that lately her back seemed curved when she was standing relaxed, but oh, I remember heartlessly adding "and it looks like you don't have a neck. . . ." Why did I have to say that anyway—I always lash out instead of just covering my head; I never lean back and let myself grow defensive in a natural way. What is it that makes me so wary of Muz and her comments and even of her life advice that proves so on-time and works like a charm to banish the barbs on each fence to my future?

This query makes my spirit sag, and I can't resist anymore it seems for a moment; I scramble for a toe-hold on renitent optimism, scramble up to the edge of it and dangle for a moment, but I'm sliding, I'm sliding backward and downward inside my outer eye where I'm eight-year-old me sidling up to Muz, bearing puny kidhood tributes, scuffling to buy out her freezeplay, her motherly non-commitment with attempted bribes of peppermint sticks, one each week at faithful allowance time, which Frozen Muz promptly sets aside to throw away. But hell, she did her best I guess, with her functional focus flat on the ground. Besides, Muz has given me a lot to be grateful for: her share of the family sass factor, and do-or-die grit. And what the heck, I'm a big girl now, all begrowned and done up in my own chunked-off life. So why's it that I can't climb for good out from under this mother-mother lugluebrication that hits the fan when my mind is turned?

After I'd left Charlie I remember how in the middle of the night or anywhere else, for solace and rapport I'd want to jump up and call Muz, or even Charlie himself for that matter. Two potentially crippling calls, but it was a time when I needed a witness and I couldn't be choosy, 'cause right then I couldn't bear to grin-talk with anyone who wasn't at the scene of my marital accident. When I met people those days I was full of bleeding gut material from once-upon-a-time, when all my madnews was just surface scum floating topside on the real-life layer. When I was some(hapless)body's wife, in a former life. (Amazing!) Once upon a time of marriage, carriage, his-and-hernias. . . . With sounds of the same nightmare chase coming from both sides of the bed.

But all I have to do now is to bring myself to speak up to Muz about my ongoing woe of having left Charlie last year; she'll understand, although in considering my problems she never discloses any comparative agony from her own experience as most people match misery with you in polite gesture of attempted shared humanity.

Yet close-mouthed as Muz is— "In case you don't know it, I'm a *private* person," she once said in irritation at my demand for personal data that she was keeping clutched to her chest— Muz is willing to share her own rooted resources with me, her only child, when the time seems ripe according to her practiced perspective. Besides, it's not her fault, that reticence; she was brought up to be close-mouthed in the deadening days of the Great Depression with its flamboyant poverty only a meal or a job away if you called attention to your dark situation. When there was no space to study at home so it was your turn finally to bring your books and tag along with your father to his stint at the country club, you knew better than to mention his working two jobs to send you and five younger brothers and sisters to teachers' college in 1936 while the rest of the world was on welfare and even whites were panicking in open desperation, though not enough to stop them from calling "Waiter!" Then, when waiterly Grandad appeared at their beck, they'd nudge each other (Is this the one with the college pretensions?) and smile "Here!" so when Grandad held out his hand, they'd slip him an open napkin of spit and chewed food to discard; and they'd watch his silent retreat from the table, then next from his job, due to mysterious layoff by the powers that were. . . .

Yet last time I really talked to Muz, I mean laid my soul bare, Muz gave her testimony right on time when I needed it in the wake of my miscarried marriage, just as I was reconsidering my move from Charlie as I continue to do in spare moments of free-floating loss. That time, when my wound was still fresh, I was convincing myself that I needed to leave Charlie for survival's sake by comparing my getaway to the way the old pioneers used to throw goods off their covered wagons when times go tough and they had to pick up speed under attack. Blip! There goes the family stove. Blam! *Fuck* this trunk of household tools! . . .

And it's still your heavy wagon time, I said to myself as I unpacked personal things at my new apartment in San Fran, delving into a box of remnants of my old life with Charlie including agonizing memorabilia such as harmless-seeming snapshot chronicles of our transient joy. Look, I thought *re* one photo, Here we are smiling in that ridiculous lowlife niteclub in East St. Lou where Charlie got so wasted he confessed that he loved me more than anything. And check it out, here's Charlie's Record (as I persisted in calling it though he gave it to me one birthday when he'd brought me no gift and I put up such a fuss)—here's Charlie's record of John Coltrane's *My Favorite Things*, that painful trickling joy of jazz in fluid process, riding on a riff of Be Here Now. . . .

Oh no, and here's Charlie's half of our honeymoon toasting goblets, our gift from Muz and Double— Look at this engraving: "Love Is The Only Elixir." (My God, but where's the antidote?) And here's our favorite teeshirt that we shared. I can't help but sniff it for illusion of comfort from Charlie's friendly body smell, then I can't help but pretend he's right here in this room, helping me unpack—he's my best friend, Charlie is, so maybe he'll help me over the hump of my lump, help me, help me manage to get over Charlie. . . .

Stop! So I use the shirt as a towel for my tears while I gather all the keepsakes and hurl them down the garbage shoot, one by clattering one. Simultaneously I'm discarding each companion memory in ritual, or so I tell myself at the scene; yet I hold onto one—I can't bear to throw away Charlie's Trane, which leaves *My Favorite Things* as all that remains of my favorite things.

I recall my attempted take-over the time Charlie said "I'll fill out my own school scholarship forms," meaning *no thanx to you*, and I can't manage to blame him; in my quest to see our two egos comfy, side by peery side (We'll get along so much better when Charlie has his bachelor's degree, I'm thinking; it'll help him withstand the grit of my wit)—in my zeal I've boiled up to the bitch point where I'm pointing out to Charlie how he never reads instructions the right way, which is from top to bott: instead he swoops onto the middle of the page and scans to the bottom, then back to the top. So I tell him how he misses and mucks up major information with his offbeat reading that's completely out of step with the data digestion process (Hup Two. . . .)

"You either swoop from the top, or you'll crip your way through on one wing," I threw out, steaming and swigging beer. "Right?" And on I roar with righteous fume, knowing full well that halo glare's malignant. It's one of those times when I can feel the Muz raging in me, can hear Double say to Muz with quiet force, "Ok, so I'm wrong! Well lead me to the guillotine!" A time when I'm caught up in the sort of needling that drives a man into the street searching for a pliant partner to override, consideration of which incenses me further, past logic and back around the spiral to bitch again.

"Well I'll do the goddamn forms myself," Charlie said then. "No, look—" he says with warning stop-still-or-I'll-stop-you look at me reaching for them anyway. So I stop, aborted and drinking a bracer of beer, noting through my fog how I'm spun back in time with Charlie to repeat-perform Muz and Double's scenes of tryst over the same basic issue. Muz and I could be a duet, singing to Charlie and to Double before he died: *I'll help you, but I'll take my just due for it!* A bitch serenade rasped from our martyring flame, as if we can't help but add char to their hard row to hoe.

Charred row to hoe, stiff way to go with no time to gather moss or rest away from strife— What a life of dry-spell disunity! Our men always versus our women. ... . Here's what I'll say to Muz about that and my role in such ingrown-type underground war: "These days . . . these days most men think I'm cold, based on my tendency to jump away from their first reach to embrace even physically," including once (and I'll keep this to myself) when I'm wearing nothing but thin see-through tee shirt and tight jeans of seeming provocation, tucked-in tease. I'm greeting a would-be beau who reaches to hug me Hello, and what I'm jumping away from really is the palpable prospect of ah, the sweet feel of his force pulsing hard deep inside me, the tart taste of my sauce on his lips, with no follow-up food for my heart that still throbs like my hotspot, with rhythms now different, no longer in sync.

But Muz (here's what I'll say about the slag that still stagnates my life)—Muz, do you see how the past has flowed forward to taint my today? Since my break made from Charlie, it seems I can never elate with full glee or be buoyed up for long by light-hearted levity. There's something holding my happiness back; something's hanging onto the hem of my bliss— Wait, let me rephrase this. . . . What is it that makes me farm through my mind in moments of soon-to-be happiness away from past woe? It seems I can't stand joy straight but have to dredge up past sadness to water it down. Most of my growth's in the past, underground; and the green clump of vigor that strangers can see (*Hey, look at me! I'm finally free!*) is merely surface-type of growth yet to be. Am I right? Muz, you tell me!

Custom-Fit Blue Genes: Scenes of the Nest

No sooner do I drop off visitant Muz at my apartment than I foment a reason to take off alone on my own, under guise of needing late-night car repair from the only moonlight mechanic I know—he's way across town natch, clear on the other side of San Fran, so's no tellin what time of night I'll manage to be back at home: this I proffer to Muz after getting her settled, having paused only long enough to snatch up my journal on the way out.

"What's that?" muses Muz with unfailing wariness, watching me doublestep past her en route to the door. She cocks her head slightly, birdlike, for better view of what it is that's under my arm— she'll add up clues soon, but meanwhile just ask, grill suspect later when crime's been detected—

looked directly in my eye while saying "that" of "What's that?"

"Oh nothing, just my journal." With quick glance to the side I toss back this nonchalant misguidance for which lightning could've struck me but overlooks its opportunity to crack open my ploy with merciless light-up of once-private truth. So seemingly spared, onward toward shadow I go with scheme still intact, said scheme being formulated crooklike by me in order to provide the wherewithal for my hasty drive here to the top of Spin Peaks where I sit now alone in the car.

Why such rush and such ruse? 'Cause what I've got with me, disguised as a mild-mannered journal, is really the answer key that I'll use to unlock the mystery of exactly what it was that forced me away from my havenly nest with the Hawk, as Charlie comes to be called in my journal, toward a blankslate future ready to chalk, my fill-in-blank future here in San Fran. As soon as I piece through the journal I can rephrase its info, its clues and its cues, into clear sunlit words that I'll tell then to Muz (and to me for that matter), so goes my reasoning and motive for the search: The journal will provide me with issues and answers and maybe a means of smooth reentry to auto-control, no matter how gruesome the orbit.

Your journal can help you learn to communicate more easily with people you know and love—yourself and other spirits from the past, who're lured through to this side of the fog by means of militant masochism, a trusty medium.

Self-induced quest that it is, to be forced toward this jolt to my spirit, jolt after jolt— In reading the journal, how can I stand the jolt of the jumps of focus that I'm famous for, with myself? Talk about free association! My personal Rorschach is a wet paint stain that could drip in all directions and usually does. When I picture reading this journal that fishes for prey in the past I see worms in a slimy can, slithering out onto terrible tangents. Wading through this journal could kill me to cure me—*It'll wash out your blood!* Yet there's no time like the present for probing the past, so open wide and take your emetic, I say to myself as if I'm a kid choke-gesting sickening tonic; open wide and swallow it down—it's good for you, you'll see!

ACTIVE INGREDIENTS: Each journal entry contains pseudoephredelirium and chlorophrenic-tremens. May contain neurotic oxides.

INDICATIONS: For temporary relief of cope congestion associated with common confusion in marital strife.

DOSAGE: To be given by single phase-of-life portion, no more than one memoir at a time. Do not exceed six doses in twenty-four hours.

WARNING: May cause excitability in sensitive persons with delusions of progress in wedlock.

Remember, "Courage itself is power!" Nevermind doubt, just do it, get to it. . . . Ok, I'll search through it, this telltale journal with its former life foibles full of Lessons To Learn, so in no time at all I'll be on my way from daily disarray to soothing understanding— "There's a reason for everything!" as Muz would say— I'll be on my way, away from San Fran as I see it glimmering below me in pinpoints of light with mobile mildspray fog wafting in from sunsetting west, away from San Fran of my now to Saint Lou of my past and soon to be mentally current. To Saint Lou,

old Saint Brew, home of Gateway Arch leading to
rows of breweries, feed mills, shoe factories, and
soft-drink distributors peddling hopeful carbonation
near steamboat strip along riverfront on the edge of
dung-colored desolate Mississippi River flowing toward escape. . . . Saint Lou of sad brick buildings
and grey-snowed internment winters followed by scald-
ing heat of merciless fry-an-egg-on-the-sidewalk sum-
mers; now-sizzling, now-frosting menopausal Saint
Lou, Midmyth hometown of auto assemblers and
aerospace designers, with steel truss bridges and rail-
roads from Wozark billyhills to downtown Old Court-
house with borrowed Dixiemyth flag and the ghost of
Ned Plot. . . . Saint Lou of my blues/internal Mississippi mud, where I walked in smoky exit footsteps of
Niggerjim and his mainboy Huck . . . where finally
last year, as I drive toward my dream of green opportune life free from strife in San Fran, I look up in the
rearview mirror at festive Three Flags amusement
park looming in soon-distant heat and I feel the parting pulse of Saint Lou's subjection to climactic ele-
ments and to her own elemental stagnation in the
capsule of time, fatal status quotidian.

Thus flow thoughts that transport me from now to
back then, days in my nest with the Hawk had come
to an end, deadlock details of which the journal will
show . . . so what next to do but to take it in hand
now and look for our ending's beginning—I'll start at
the top of last year.

I'M CONSIDERING HOW THE HAWK WALKS
STRAIGHT TOWARD HIS MEDSKOOL GOAL
THROUGH WINDS OF STINGING RACE-HATE

*though he's troopless all the while, with no family back-
ground for backup troops to sustain him on his trek. And
look at me as inside instigator, all the time whining for his
love, dealing him one more dull demand despite his need for
a second line of defense;* instead of support I add yet another
no comprende *to his tactical efforts—this from faithful
should-be better-half.* "Love me, love me," i continue to
whine when hell, this is war where love's just an added
attraction on the order of Reena Lorne entertaining WWII
troops under fire. Can't i dig it? —Love's a temporary
anesthetic to be used when needed to soft salve your war
wounds. So, Grow up! I keep telling myself. Be woman
enough to take your rightful place as Reena for this warrior
with no further plaint!*

Thus the spirit struck so that the Hawk and I made
love for the first time in eons which may be berserk,
but it's one of the hidden glues of our marital bond,
the way the Hawk brings me to spasms of waves in
wild ripples, shivering prickles to the point where he
can just lie still and laugh, it's ok—

*Hey Hawk, look at me—i'm shooting from spot to spot on
sparks of your current . . . my legs clamp your back/help me
cling to your coil . . . connecting outlet to line-in exactly in
phase . . . Now crossover magnets . . . Wait! Don't you
move!*

I'm loving the Hawk tremendously when my bliss
bubble turns shitful all on its own, causing an ooze of
I bet he thinks I don't love him! But no, he doesn't think
in slippery subtlety; the Hawk's thoughts are concrete slabs chiseled chronologically and objectively
with demarcated borders in between, unlike my own
amoeba slotch from point to point. Ah, but that's
why we fit. . . .

I'm still smiling when I get my second paranoid prick: *Suppose the Hawk's deliberately using me down to a spark so his own ego-beam can shine in my shadow? We all could use a shadow. . . .*

Aw, don't be paranoid, I think at the time; yet aren't we all so paranoid now that the only real transition between our passages, the only continuity between our panicky personal paragraphs is polymer paranoia—splice glue that pastes our puzzle pieces into a collective point of view. Paranoia's our only plot line, and it eats away out theme of existence through random corrosion, a built-in deficiency. We oughta be warned—

DO NOT USE THIS GLUE TO BOND EGOS! CAN CAUSE SEVERE MIND INJURY! IF SUBSTANCE COMES INTO CONTACT WITH COPE-ABILITY, RUSH TO NEAREST EMERGENCY FACILITY, DISCARDING LEAKY SELF-IMAGE EN ROUTE IN THE MANNER OF ANY SENSIBLE SURVIVOR OF ANY OTHER DISASTER.

Yet later, after this convincing, I catch myself mumbling "I love him but I hate him," sawing back and forth against dull rusty hostility toward the Hawk, a discovery that rattles all my beams at once and drives me straight into ego root shelter.

THE HAWK AND I LOOK LIKE BROTHER AND SISTER—SO MUCH ALIKE that when he slides off into one of his sulks/deep hole silentathons, or when he doubleclutches into Heapbig Macho Me ("There's only one man in this house," he explains, requiescat in pace)—i look at him/at me: tan-skinned ectomorph/tall&thin, w/ big dark eyes of surprise and my lips fuller w/moustache newly grown on tap . . . at my chin, rockier, & my eyebrows furrier, & i've shot up from five-seven to six-one. . . . This nature study's gone all out of whack; part of me has pinched off protozoan style & grown into its own tho the hookup to its host is still there.

With this last journal entry comes formative insight that seems to rush up and lunge at me: part of the problem between me & the Hawk may have been over-identification with each other which made for a weird double dose of our hopes and our fears from which we o.deed. Could it be? Let me see, I'll read on. . . .

BLESSED BE THE BANAL, FOR THEY SHALL INHERIT THE EARTH AND ALREADY HAVE: I've just finished writing the Hawk's Personal Statement for his Lewisnclark School of Medicine application, despite both odds to the contrary: baby chick Mia's timely two-year-old's addenda while i'm creating my tale, and the hump of my choke when i think what if this app makes the grade and the Hawk's accepted to Lewisnclark U. here in St. Brew? *We'll wind up nesting here for the rest of our terms, a pitiful payoff that seems so like punishment— But never-mind, we've got to apply to all three schools of our choice, it's MEDSCAPP procedure; you pays your bread, you takes your test and applies, applies and reapplies, w/ no thot for personal pref or distractions of the sort—if a school takes you, you'll take it; that's understood, it's for your own good, so hush your sniveling subjectivity, just go on and rap on each app as if it's your foremost and craven desire, e.g.:*

*LEWISNCLARK U. IS MY PRIMARY CHOICE BE-
CAUSE (1) I WAS BORN AND REARED IN SAINT
LOU AND AM FAMILIAR WITH L&C'S SCHOLASTIC
RESOURCES HERE [. . . .] (2) MY WIFE, AN L&C
ALUMNA, HAS SEVERAL JOB OFFERS WHICH WOULD
SUSTAIN US FINANCIALLY WHILE I ATTEND MED-
ICAL SCHOOL AT LEWISNCLARK UNIVERSITY [. . . .]
(3) I HAVE HAD A WEALTH OF REWARDING EXPE-
RIENCES IN THE COURSE OF MY OFF-CAMPUS BAC-
CALAUREATE RESEARCH, MOST OF WHICH WAS
COMPLETED VIA THE RESOURCES AND FACILI-
TIES OF LEWISNCLARK UNIVERSITY. . . .*
Now ain't dat what de folks like to hear?

I remember it all, can see it today as sort of a play
still in progress back then on our usual set, with all
the missed cues still standard, the same:

The Hawk, after reading the app, then completed:
"What does any of this extra stuff have to do with my
application?"

Me: " 'Extra stuff'?"

The Hawk (with lip curled: No noise.)

Me: "The detail, you mean?"

The Hawk (with clench-jaw patience, staring straight
ahead).

Me: "Well see, your personal statement is the real
meat of your app." (He smiles.) "You have to person-
alize the thing—you know, into yourself and your
goals while you speak to key checkpoints on the
reviewing committee's hidden agenda." (The Hawk's
grin wriggles a moment then fades, yet do I stop?
No, I go on:) "The reviewing committee'll be a broth-
erhood of WASP status-quomen see, and we have to
show that you fit into their bag of tradition in all but

one minor, so-what meaning way—" (Uh oh, now the Hawk's looking to kill; somehow I've activated his hatred of being left out of the ways and means of achievement-sucess, which he thinks is all by design, a thumping paranoia, so I decide to sound less didactic; I'll say this is my own humble opinion and no more.)

"Well, I'm convinced that the packaging counts," I say to the Hawk with a smile. (But no sale, from the looks of the Hawk, and now here's my other foot in it . . . what can I say? I know, keep it general:) "Well, it's this kind of detail that sets you off from the next joker who's Qualified Too. As I see it at least." (I tack on this modest finale as soon as it flares to mind, and yep, ok, it's cool or at least it's the end—the Hawk's walking away, but tact and good timing elude me as usual; I can't help but rush to catch him and say, "Will we have a problem finding a place to live if one of the other schools takes you and we move away from St. Lou, do you think?"

"Not if I know you," the Hawk says with a side-twisted grin. "You'd push your way into the Taj Mahal."

"I don't know about that," I stretch-smile to say. "What I meant was—"

"I *know* what you meant," the Hawk slices in. "What *I* mean is if you're asking if we'd ever be in Blood's situation." ("Blood" being one of a group of black L&C medstudents, the school's total affirmative action battalion from six thousand students— Blood with his pregnant wife who'd succumbed to living at a local YMCA due to "lack of available married students' housing," or so he was told by L&C U. when he arrived from a small town down south. Then after a year, said medstude still was living at the Y, and financial survival for him and his family was working nights after school, a move which made him subject to fine or the axe, since the medskool *school's* your gig, with overtime at that, so anything else is outlawed. Meanwhile tho, Blood still was waiting for his fork-tongued financial aid to materialize, holding his breeaatthhh til it came, which it never did but yep, in the void the axe came instead—it's always prompt and dependable.)

It's this critical case that the Hawk decides I must be alluding to now so therefore goes on to respond, "It could happen, but it wouldn't, not with you at the helm of our steering committee."

What can I say? "I'm strong willed."

"So I see!" the Hawk says to me. "Look, this is no big deal really, people make too much of it." He turns and looks into distance. "Medschool is *school*; it's a means to an end. You do what you've got to do, that's all, wherever you get to do it."

Which sounds like something Vole would say, I can't help but think as I watch the Hawk's squared back shoulders recede from my view— I thought this vaguely back then, with pitiful absence of perception, though now I can see that the Hawk was single-minded when it came to achievement; which is why his goal would come to pass; here at this pivotal point was a clue to resolving the mystery of his riddling one-trackitis which seemed to be routed right under my skin.

Then too in recall I can see how the Hawk must have hated the thought of his upcoming move into medskool, hated the move in itself due to congenital conservatism, his tucked-in nature which he can't correct all alone on his own any more than, say Vole can help hers—both of their childhoods were hard, and conservatives still need their childhoods so they can let grow.

Also the Hawk must've been stunned with fear for his *self* in the course of his upcoming gruel through gringo medskool— There was nothing in his past to prep him for imminent shock of being cast among pale preppies on their homey home turf. It was anticipated initiation of a caustic solo sort that concerned the Hawk, or so it seems now to me—he must have feared, *If I go through medskool and come out alive, I might not leave with the self I brought in.* . . . There was more evidence of this probably, evidence of his fear of integration on the outside and simultaneous disintegration on the inside; if so I should have dug it— I've been there, at schools where my grades were lousy for example, 'cause integration alone was a full-time fringeless job— When I got home from school all I wanted to do was to rest and be black, homework be damned, just be cool and be black and kick back for a few, I mean Whew! I'd been *F'd* when I should've been *A'd*; "You *couldn't* have written this," teachers would say, and since Vole and Double never'd had the fate to integrate, what did they understand or know about the close-burn ague of it? What's more, white students didn't care; they'd just stare, *Look at you!* And black students, the few, would assimilate from view as prestoically as they could, would look away when they saw you so as not to see themselves *sans* plaster persona; so who could I turn to, when nobody knowed the trouble I seed . . . nobody knew what it *be like*. . . .

"Do you hear me, young lady?" Vole said to me when I got home from school on the day that school got home before me via a call from the principal. This was the day I'd been tried, convicted, and suspended from grade school, and *good*, I thought then with reckless satisfaction, it's about time; I've had it up to over my head with Sacred Sacrament School and its casual curse of *Welcome, little nigs, but now stay in your place we've got here for you*. Already at ten I've fought a lifetime of frustrating wars, already I'm a disabled vet of desegregation. What's more, I've been tricked into this fray with no warning of the hell of it *(I integrate, you integrate, he, she, or it integrates, then we all disintegrate)*— So farewell and forget you, Two-Faced Sacrament School! Goodbye and good riddance to you and your penance—

"Are you listening to me?" Vole said, and already she'd started to answer herself: "Well you'd better listen, and hear me well because I don't care *what* Sister said to you or how she said it, or what the other kids said, or *any* of that jive— There's no excuse for talking back to your teacher. And using curse words too? Have you lost your fifth grade mind?"

"One word, Vole," Double cut in. "The word was 'ass,' which is a lukewarm cuss word if I ever heard one. Let's get the story straight—"

"There are a billion arbitrary circumstances you can pull out of your hat to rationalize a situation like this," said Muz. "So where do you draw the line?"

My voice trembled when I spoke and the next thing I knew, I'd begun to cry with anger against my will, treacherous tears betraying me, damn! "You don't understand, Vole! She said, Sister Jude said I must have copied my whole book report, cuz it was too good to be true! She called me up to her desk in front of everybody—"

("An that's when you let her have it!" said the runaway rascal who lived in my mind. "In front of everybody! 'You want the truth?' you said. 'Well I slaved over a hot library to write this thing, so I *know* I did it. And fact *is*, I don't give a gnat's ass *what* you think!' Jude turned three shades darker than purple!")

"You were *wrong*, young lady," Vole said. "You've got more nerve than the law allows."

"Now wait, Vole," Double looked down at me and shook his head. I thought I detected a glint of his smile, but I couldn't be sure.

"*You* wait," Vole told him. "That's your main problem. You've been waiting all your life!"

"The point is," Double said in his slow careful drawl, "is the child gonna learn to speak up for herself, or is she gonna tapdance through life? Let her stand up for her convictions, so that—"

"You stand when it's *time* to stand!" Vole sliced in. "You don't make a stand at the edge of a cliff! Getting suspended from schools defeats *her*, not this nun, Sister whoever she is. The nun already has her education . . . and my child is going to have *hers*. In case it's slipped your mind, she has a one-time opportunity here, going to a school of this caliber. And when opportunity knocks, you snatch it in by the hand!" Muz paused and turned to me. "Don't *try* me now.

We're going to Sacred Sacrament Elementary School tomorrow, and you're going to tell Sister you're sorry you cursed, and—"

With this last, I can't help it, I cry out in outrage at the shocking prospect of taking low in public, giving scandal to all my fearless friends—

"Now wait a minute, Vole," Double said meanwhile, but Vole kept up her forward march to the drum of her own priorities. ". . . You're going to say that you're sorry you lost your temper in the classroom, and it won't happen again!"

In desperation I went over to Double. "If you could see how full of pride Sister Jude is, Double! Tellin us how proud she is to be servin God among the colored! Says she doesn't consider it a sacrifice at all, she just offers it up!"

"See?" Double said to me. "You natives just never know how to be grateful, that's all. An the missionaries won't stand for that!"

"That's right, laugh it off," said Vole with one hand on her hip. "Show the child how it's done."

But Double leaves Vole to sputter to herself and continues to me, "Sugar, there'll always be stiff-minded folks doin their best to puncture your power, which in your case is all of your talents, includin the way you think things through better than a lot of hardheaded grownups—"

"Oh sure," Vole said to me. "Congratulations on your insolence. And on your timing too. Keep it up!" Then, after a moment she put her hand on my shoulder and looked down into my eyes. "Look," she said, "I know you think I'm rough on you."

("That's right," said my rascal.)

"But I'm only trying to pave the way for you up ahead. You don't realize it now, but it pays to be fully prepared to hold your own in any circumstances— and Lord knows this is not an all-black world! Look how good I was in school at your age. Who knows *what* I could have done if I had had your advantages." She paused again. "Your father means well, but I can't understand him," she said this as if Double's not right smack there in the room, so I look over at him—he's looking away—and Vole follows my gaze, addressing Double now who gradually turns to face her—he can tell she's talking to him by her tone of vibe.

"You seem to want it so the child is comfortable now and completely unprepared to compete in the future," Vole said to Double. "You don't get but so many chances in this world! When one comes your way, you don't have the luxury of a tailor-made fit, you just grab the thing and put it on, upside down, inside out, you name it!"

"Now you know I'm not the Tomish type," she went on. "You *know* I'm not." (And yep, I have to agree instantly, already I've seen and heard Vole brandishing her blackness in many a critical face-to-face confrontation where she could have tucked it in for ease and comfort of maneuver. On the other hand, I've also seen Vole readjust her normal speech pattern so as to appear to be white on the telephone when she called police, medical services, repairmen, and even sales people at department stores— It garnered respect and cleared the confusion before it began, she said.)

"I *am* a pragmatist though," Vole went on, "and

I'm no fool." Here she stopped to give a short sour laugh. "I'm not silly enough to let anybody knock me off my track at their whim. Or at their set-up, for that matter." She looked away in silence for a moment, mysteriously it seemed, although now I realize she was considering tricks and barriers she'd hurtled in her past in order to get ahead, fiery hoops she'd had to jump through again and again in the long-distance race with her loaded baton and bigots in the woodpile all down the stretch.

Double it seemed had no answer for this last from Vole, or at least he was silent—disgustingly so I thought at the time, when he belonged in my corner, championing my defense and consequent release from life in prison at Sacred Sac with its flak, a wracking proposition which causes me to tug at Double's hand and lace my fingers through his so that he'll look down at me and smile; and when he does this, instead of boomerang-smiling in return I stare back at him with the fury of my seriousness and consternation. It's then that he leans over to whisper to me (and by peeking around the side of his face I can see Vole's wordless getaway from the room): "Don't ever lose your smile— And I don't mean like this." (Here he flashed a wide Tom-type grin.)

"What I'm sayin is never let *anybody* make you lose the gift of your smile. It's the magic gift the gods gave the warrior in every fable there is. It can let you do anything, be anything, and come home to yourself under damn near any circumstances. In that class-room back there with the short-sighted teacher, it was time for your smile when she started her stuff, 'cause that was your cue that the circus was ready to start. Where you went wrong was in thinkin you had to jump in the ring along with the clown. Next time, just keep to the sidelines an smile at the act!"

It was in this way, with Double's advice and consent, that I came to swallow chagrin and to flex with the system of school's twisted lessons, although "Smile at the act"—this rankled something inside me and continued to rub, up til the time of Double's death in my teenhood. There are times when smiling ought to be outlawed, I thought to myself, and before this I'd've sworn he'd agree. Some times were times for "strategic retreat," Double said though, when it's best to pack up your short-range plans and put em on the shelf.

"Fact is," he said, "this tactic's almost always the way in a short vs. long johns situation, where even though shorts or short plans feel comfortable when the sun's on your side and long johns might itch you while there's warmth around, don't you forget that long plans stand you in good stead through the chill times, and chill times are predominant. Even surface-minded folks have sense enough to know the earth's getting colder by degrees!"

So due to this maxim, and because of the antarctic climate back then and again later in life with the Hawk in St. Brew, what I should do now is to don my long-john thoughts here in the journal. . . . After all, it's stood me in good stead through at least one winter, the season of its engenderment, and it's only itched me on special occasions, when I failed to take note of its doubleknit pattern, or when times grew warm without warning. I remember that winter in Saint Brew, winter of my malcontent when cloistered by climate, all I could do was to hole up and write the Hawk's apps; I'd look at the Tube for relief, only pausing to care for LC, the Little Chicadee as I'd begun to call Mia, or to take time to note in my journal:

TV'S ALL OVER ME LIKE FORMALDEHYDE, & *I'm waking at three/four-hour intervals w/ the sound of a* *video voice ringing off my eardrums—till finally, at three* A.M. there's the final wake-up to the starspangled jest, just to see if you're paying attention, you dregs of the melting pot. (Our inside images are double-duty, built to convert vidicon white into black&related, i.e. our self-image negative becomes positive after conversion of contrast factors. $W - B \rightarrow B + /W$.) The Tube— it's my comic relief w/ its neo-stymies superspades mushy-mammies redhot-mulattas & sitcom Toms— Now that's entertainment! No pain; I don't feel a thing. Cerebral rasterscan leaves no tracks. Well maybe a minor adjustment in point-of-view. An after-effect that's barely perceptible.

It was a winter of snowbound decision, that winter in which I produced my plan of how to manage our move to San Fran where the Hawk would go to medical school. (*"You'll see!"* I thought then about doubters-to-be)— We'd manage to move to San Fran of my ongoing vigorous dream, about which I yearned in the journal:

A FREEFORM RUMINEE, THAT'S ME! When I *dive off into my beer I cd be anywhere at all. . . . I'm lifted* *off the boggedown ground & up into clouds of vitality* *drifting toward Lotusland, home of poppies & pansies w/rivers* *of goldust rushing from Los Diablos in her south to fogfilled* *northstar San Fran, where I land and I ride the waves of the hills in this beercan, no fear, my grace is amazing, and I'll drink to that!*

That's it, I thought then in that final winter and first year of marriage during which I boozed and cruised toward my own personal dream under guise of propelling the Hawk toward his goal of entry to medskool, 'though then, at the time, I'd yet to admit this, thinking only *I'll manage to move yet to San Fran, where there's freedom to be & freedom for me far away from Saint Brew with its clean constipations that block up my soul! I'll take the frontier, and the wilder the better's the way that I see it! My covered wagon's been packed all my life & I'm ready to roll here/there/any goddamn where but the spot where I'm freezing. . . . Other side of the fence, take me! Come on, fold me right up in your green opportune dream!*

What's more, I thought then, the Hawk'll dig our move too; he'll see and understand later—which should've been a clue as to how it takes two to tango in a plan of this type— One marital partner never can plan alone for the other and hope to succeed with a one-sided deed; but not knowing this then I fomented tall foam-headed plans and gulped em straight down with a secretive grin, proceeding to write medskool apps and app supps for the Hawk with prehensile emphasis on apps for the U. of San Span without the Hawk's knowledge, consent, or interference— I couldn't risk his grounded view; he'd only hold us back or down too close to ground! Besides, his was not to reason why; *just do your do* while *I* apply. . . .

PROLONNNGED TENSION (the screech, in your mind, of dentist's drill on shivering tooth): it's the anyday-nowness

90

*of the Hawk's selection for interview at the U. of San Span
that sets me on edge while I wait for notification by pony
express mail. If only we could look forward to a definite
cut-off point in this selection process, but no, this sickening
wait for notification is part of the rites of admission, so just
pop antacid and shut your gaseous flow. . . .*

*But I can't keep still, I keep thinking, IF ONLY THE
HAWK'S ACCEPTED TO THE U. OF SS!—I can't
help but dream this possible dream; it's my sole hope of
transplant to fertile surroundings far from quicksand Saint
Brew. . . .*

*It's driven by this outlook that I go on to write in
response to the following:*

Q: "WHY DO YOU NEED THIS SCHOLARSHIP?"

*A: A SCHOLARSHIP TO THE U. OF SAN SPAN
WOULD HELP ME TO FINANCE AN OTHERWISE
FINANCIALLY PROHIBITIVE PROFESSIONAL EDU-
CATION AND WOULD PUT ME ON FINANCIAL PAR
WITH MY FELLOW STUDENTS FOR THE FIRST
TIME. (WHILE ATTENDING UNDERGRADUATE
SCHOOL ON A FULL-TIME BASIS, I WORKED FULL-
TIME AS A MACHINE SHOP ASSISTANT AT OVERT
BEARINGS, INC.) . . .*

*THE SCHOLARSHIP WOULD ALLAY MUCH OF THE
ADDITIONAL STRESS TO WHICH I HAVE BEEN
SUBJECT, ALLOWING ME TO CONCENTRATE MY
ENERGIES FULLY ON THE PURSUIT OF MY EDU-
CATIONAL OBJECTIVE. . . .*

*Now let me re-read the whole thing, so I can assess
&project.*

Let's see, basal bootstrap thrust—check: kneegrow edu-cated& responsible, now ready for rocket propulsion; cosmic ray counter—check; gamma ray counter, heavy particle counter, impulse magnetometer, ultra-v detector: a.o.k. Our salvo's in trajectory and ready to launch, from a lowly Saint Brew ghetto to stars of a medskool—from Midmyth's slums down here in inner earth, Demomyth's inner earth, to casual coastal clouds of success. Turbojet up and away!

A sure-fire escape— What refuge there seemed up ahead in my scheme, at least as I planned it! Yet best laid plans of mice and men gang aft agley, astray, and every whichway but how we planned em, which proves that planning's inane, it's based on insuffi-cient evidence when we're mindless of coming detrac-tions ahead. Yet I wasn't alone in my folly, the Hawk had his potent plans too which he shared in an un-likely gush, almost rushing to tell me—this after five days of his silence and absence, I remember it well; all of a sudden he had Something To Tell, a strange-ness tied up with more strangeness, about which I wrote in the journal, noting twisted developments in order received. . . .

COLD FRONT ASIDE, THE FROSTY HAWK DOTH TALK: His Genetics Seminar today dealt with theory and practice of Big4 University's prizewinning physicist who maintains that blacks are genetically inferior to whites. (Is you SHO, Cap'n suh?) Apparently we've been limping through the diaspora handicapped all along by our own topheavy right brain lobes (Rhythm&Artistry Division: shuffle shuffle tap tap, heeheehee)—as opposed to whites who're endowed, it happens, with cornfed left lobes of studlike proportions.

(And just to think: All those rational faubustians & kookoo klansfolks here in Midmyth and next door in Dixiemyth and on the rising rampage in dawn's early light all over the home of the free, and we never appreciated their teachings, disabled lobers that we are. But quitters never win, and empirical labs are never too late, so we still can take a lesson from those rational yankeemythians in Mayflower City. See them with their wise olde brickbats enlightening schoolbuses with young black rhythm inside?)

Don't get me started— It was at the end of said semester when the Hawk was sitting still in shadowy shock that he was approached by oil-smiling Dr. A, his Genetics proff who sees the Hawk as a fascinating pet mutate who defies his meager dark origins. Dr. A told the Hawk that he must be crazy not to have applied to Latter Day U. in Seasalt City (where the Hawk could be accepted, heaven hip us, to medskool in lily-whiteland, home of the insular Boremans and other such welcoming groups).

"If you manage to get into Latter, it'll put the U. of Saint Lou on the map," said Doc A. "'We send our pre-med students to schools like L.U.,' we could say then. You should send those applications far and wide! Don't be NIGGARDLY with em!" he said with a smirk as he made for the door. . . .

"Now wait just a peckerwood minute!" the Hawk should've said then, but nope, he'd never say that; he'll push straight ahead to his Goal come hell or bad-news bigots— "Just forge ahead," he says and indicates with deeds. Also, and furthermore—but wait, enough of speculation, let me climb back on my point, which is that the Hawk's now planning to call Latter Day U. claiming that he hasn't heard from them since applying six weeks ago, before their application

deadline, after which "They'll check their files, apologize, and ask me to send them a 'second' application," grinned the Hawk.

Now here was a cue, I can see it today, of how the Hawk was willing to work wild means to the end which he'd set for himself; he wasn't uncreative, just spare with creativity—he used it as a spare for driving special surfaces. I wish I'd seen it then, we could've chauffered side by side in tandem, not at odds. Survival, afterall, is a crisis built for two.

AND MOVING RIGHT ALONG TO WRONG, our rent check bounced, along with our grocery store floater—both hit the mud with a thud. What's more, our note's due on the loan to buoy us over the application fee flood and up to the edge of the interview reef of schools on our list, the loan being finance company standard 30% interest, but anybody's eligible for it, no matter your credit or suspectful source of income, says this "equal opportunity lending institution"—just step right up and be burned.

It was this conflagration which led to our whatelse-but-need to call on Vole and her trusty pocketbook, a realization which somehow sludges to mind how I'd convinced myself that I didn't give a damn about Vole's feelings about what I was doing with what I had to offer. . . .

"Vole, I know what I'm doing with my commitments to mothering the Chick and back-throne driving the Hawk"—I still can hear myself growling this theme through the phone when I'd called Vole *re* the bread and instead she'd exhorted me to salvage myself.

"Put your feet on the ground! Think of *you* as Number One!" she'd yelled at me in a motherly way, causing me to chafe endodermally, erupting with thoughts of *Well thanx for the tip from your own modus operandus*; I can see where I've failed to follow my leader. . . .

But Vole never takes heed of grumbling silence around her, she severs straight through it, no muss. "Just look at it this way," she said to my seethe. "You come from a long line of women, *good looking* women who knew how to use what they had. And honey, we've got a lot of grey matter and the spunk to apply it, with or without a man who understands, though they could be our weak spot, I'll grant you that. But you, look at you— You've got all the right stuff in you, or could have at least—but you need like *hell* to learn how to work it!"

It's the start of new dues owed to Vole, 'though little do I know it then (which's all the best for my sanity's sake 'cause anxietywise I'm running on full)— See here what I wrote in the journal:

WELL HERE WE ARE, ME&MY BEER on the backporch so the Chick can sleep, which is an apt example of these three rooms and their blues. . . . Today's my birthday (ooh-wah), and there's no note of my presence, less birth from the Subthermal Hawk. . . .

"You took up the whole day with the car yesterday," he explained on his way through the hall.

"Well today is today, so I don't see why we can't just bop over all that and do something to celebrate, just for a minute. . . ."

I smiled with all my might, feeling off-cue with more stress still due cuz we'd planned, or I'd planned for us to go see "Man In the Marigolds" at the U. of

Saint Brew later that nite, it's to be our first date in six months to which the Hawk had agreed weeks ago. But nevermind my upraised hope, this scheme of my dreams would turn back into a pumpkin yet. Back into a pumpkin . . . now I'm inside its shell. . . . *He put her in a pumpkin shell, and there he kept her very.* . . . Hell! I've had it by now, and fate's well aware of that fact, but. . . .

"I changed my mind," said the Hoar-Headed Hawk. "I'm too busy to go the show." Then comes his whistling and he heads for the bathroom where he cranks down the metal bathtub stopper and turns on the faucets full blast so doesn't hear me when I exit stage right, driving away in our favorite prop.

Thus in little or no time I'm with my curses at Vole's house, where all's never lost completely; she keeps a survival ratskeller of Cutty Shark and remedies of a feather that beat the hell out of stuffed-chicken soup. And though Vole may not be what you'd call domestically inclined, I feel so at home when I've waded through her tumbleweed dust and newspaper fossils from 1322—they're still waiting in the livingroom just as they were in my kidhood, untouched and yellowly sanctified. What's more, there's Vole herself in her judging robe and slippers, always ready for friendly debate, pacing the floor in her vigilant zeal just as she was then when once, at seventeen and still in an innocent gangster youth, I'm hanging up the phone with its message of upcoming mayhem:

"Quick, Vole! *J* says he's coming straight here with a gun! Ain't nothin gonna stop him, he sez—"

And Vole grabs my shoulders: "Nothing *is* going to

stop him," she rasps. "Take care to watch out for those verbs!"

Points of View: They wriggle all over each other with no thought for harmony of thrust, like my attitude toward Muz—she's the mother-hate figure in my Freudian past; I'm black with a glen-plaid mother, integration freak, bourgeoisie to her hilt. . . .

But Muz, well there's this further side of her that's so sad; she was overlooked in her own family of six desperates growing up during the Great Depression. Heartwrenching, the way her mother shined her on—

"Now look," Muz shot at me once, "you think I failed you. Well I want you to know, my mother failed me!"

What could I say? Poor Muz, overlooked and under-mothered while the Deed was getting done, their family deed: Grampa Megloe working his two gigs, waiting his tables on the U.S. Admiral, the Sadie Hawkins, and the Huckleberry Finn, riverboating up and down the redneck Mississippi while Mother Rose-mary's busy grinding the kids (except for Kate who's deep in her books, tucked away on her own in a corner somewhere, completely involved in her own course of study)—Mother Rose's grinding the kids through her ad-hoc pep-and-prep school back in the kitchen and to heck with the Depression. The whole sacrifice is to gear them for their Education, their racism-release; it would change the whitefokes' whole point of view; presto, their onionskin wands would be good for color synchronicity. The Megloe kids would all go to college . . . and they did of course, with Uncle One's feat of a doctorate and Vole's own *coup* of a master's, a miracle, at least to the eye, external dynamics. . . .

I can see Muz a few years ago, telling how she'd broken news of the Hawk's switch to his pre-med major to a co-worker at social services and the woman had jabbed, "Well tell your daughter to be sure to keep up with her husband"; so with no further ado Muz unfurled lauds of our own family crest, telling me later, "Well hell, she was way off base, so I had to get her told. We're brilliant, that's all there is to it! Brilliance runs in the family, from your great-grandfather [graduated from Dixiemyth State in 1843 under guise of whiteness, then snapped back to black] down to Uncle One [with his pre-WWII doctorate at Segregate U.]."

Well let's see, I thought in response, we're sure miserable enough to be geniuses if that's any indication—frustrated, enraged, and magnetized to toxic mates; haven't figured out how to live out our lives, duhhh— But anyhow, despite all that, I'm only part them and mainly me, only one-third Megloe; one-third Megloe, one-third Double's clan, and one-third original me, the latter root being the long thick radicle trailing from my own sapling out into the world's onshifting sod.

Seed, sod, I'm only a pod of our knarl-rooted thick-trunky family tree about which I wrote in my ongoing register, but first came news with regard to my nuptial nest. . . .

BECAUSE OF THE XMAS HOLIDAYS WE'RE HELD IN SUSPENDED ANIMATION by the post office, though next month should bode tidings from schools which intend to interview the Hawk, including foremostly U.S.S. in promising Lotusland "out on the coast" as they say, on the west coast of bliss in the end zone of Demomyth's kick-off intent. . . . then, after interview & subsequent selection, we'll know by Spring how to plan our move, whether to think cross-country or crosstown. And what's there to say? I hate to digest it, but so far it's likely the Stuffbound Hawk'll choose to go to Lewisnclark U. due to its Burn Research Unit he says (and further due to his own nestful nature, the Hawk being extremely reluctant to risk and roam. Call it aneurism of the Big Move vein, compared to guess who, who can fly out so far that it's hard to get back. . . .)

And that's how I felt then for real; it's easy to spread your wingspan from home in the nest, not so fun to rise and try to fly alone in an urb with a pummet under your feathers as I learned later head-bumptly, but more of that anon—enough of heretofore hindsight, just retract your lens and read on. . . .

HELL MUST CONSIST OF AN ONGOING ROUND OF FAMILY RE-UNIONS where inmates are fed eggnog and fruitcake every hour on the hour. That's right, you Megloes heard me, I'm determined not to go to the Megloe family bash New Year's eve!

"But when will we get to see you?" said Aunt Megloe in invitation. "You keep yourself so scarce!"

Which is true, so i do stay away from in-clan rivalry and corrosive jealousy that eats through ferrous barriers to generation-gap booby traps in which the younger generation can never prevail—although truth be told, there is a certain strength of elders' ambition and consequent sacrifice to be gained from Meglo re-union, and unity begins at home. The family that fights together endures together cuz blood is thicker than weariness. Hence, since kin is sanguine, i owe the Megloes respect for their trials and forerunners' tribs on behalf of my generation's far easier/less colorfast access to success, so maybe i should go, just freeze my ire and trudge thru the snow. . . . *But no, i've had it up to here with their fights fueled by Cutty Shark; you Megloes set a bad example—well you used to set a bad example, now you set a bad opportunity for me to booze and fume in your image and likeness when all i want is to get your role models off my runway, at least for the moment— Just leave me alone in my blue genes!*

WELL, *OK,* WOMAN'S HOME, *I'VE COOKED MY XMAS DINNER.* . . .

(When I read this now, I recall the time Muz suddenly took it upon herself to cook a family meal for the first time; I was about twelve at the time and shocked speechless, thinking *Muz hates a lot of ado so I'll just say nothing, just walk on outside and recover alone.* . . . Then when I get back, without a word she meaningfully sets down a big bowl brimming with tuna salad. *Ok—I get it,* I think; I'll play this through impromptu, so still silent, I go to the bathroom to wash my hands and return to the table to find when I dip in my fork that ugh, in her search for green vegetable filler, Muz's used canned squish-green peas, now swimming in a sea of viscous mayonnaise. So I brace myself for *mal appetit.* . . . But nevermind Muz and her stab at domestication, just go back to notes of my own wedlock deadlock. . . .

WELL, *OK,* WOMAN'S *HOME, I'VE COOKED MY XMAS DINNER, and it's a good one from recipes pieced together from family friends and soul food cookbooks, no thanks to no-cooking Muz (yet what are successive generations for but to correct the errors of our elderesses?). . . .*

I've cooked mashed turnips with salt pork, candied sweets, dressing with oysters, oyster stew, mixed greens w/ ham hocks, corn bread, mince pie, and sweet potatoe pie. . . . And am i finally gettin gdrunk, sthoned, wrent, broiled & skewed, on 2-Star Rennesy cognac to be exact. Hell, i myself am a human flaming dessert and good! excerpt my flingers won't work so hot noy (sp?), so it's time for comminucation in another morde or mode.

"SO WHAT'S THE BIG DEAL?" said the Siberian Hawk when he flew thru home for a moment, meaning Xmas is only a pre-fab commercial excuse to get you caught up in a fever of the pocketbook; adults should know better, which must be why he's taken the opportunity to get back in the street this Xmas evening too, on the way once again to his mysteries in the biochem lab so that i'm home alone with blissful-ignorant Mia/"LC," the Lil Chickadee. We're singing Kwanzaa carols and baking Xmas cookies (red & lotsa green) when suddenly, within minutes of the Hawk's exit the doorbell rings. The second-thought Hawk without his key? i think with a desperate flare of Welcome back! But no, it's his mother, the Buzzard, of all kringles, standing here in our doorsill snow right on morbid cue; now she's in the kitchen.

"Well? Where's my Xmas gift?" she says.

And we look at each other. . . . Stalactites could grow in our vibe; her eyes narrow to clench & lynch me on the spot and i shoot back a screaming silent communiqué: Lady, have you noticed how i can't stand to be in the same deadly kitchen with you? How i run from the knives? How i jump from the cleaver?

AT-ISSUE MEMORANDUM CONTESTING ASSIGNMENT OF MOTHER-IN-LAW

I DO SOLEMNLY SWEAR THAT THE MOTHER-IN-LAW IN QUESTION IS OUT OF THE QUESTION.
Case closed. Now all we need is the noose for defendant.
(But realife loves an anti-climax, so the following month the Buzzard winds up working (at) the post office around the corner, and yep, that's me over there taking her home-cooked dinner on Sundays due to threats from the Hawk: his silence and sulkathon.)
Make that the noose for two.

". . . WELL DO YOUR PARENTS VALUE EDU-CATION?" This question was shot at the Hawk by quizzative Dr. A at school yesterday.
"Well, my mother does in a way," said the Hawk, meaning or should be meaning on your own, that is— *the Buzzard having maintained an outlook of* once you're seventeen you're on your own, my son, *hasta lluega. . . .*

When I think of the Buzz I remember the ninth month of my pregnancy, that fraught-filled month in a Saint Lou summer of heat that sucks your breath away—it vacuums up your energy and energy to be— when up pops the Hawk's missing mother, who calls to pre-order a grandchild of a specific spitting image: her own.

"Just thought I'd let you know, I hope the baby's brown-skinned," said the Buzz to me over the phone. "I don't want no *yella* grandbaby now" (meaning light tan-skinned like me and her Hawk-son).

"Uh, hello?" I picture the Buzzard muck-rake grin-

102

ning at her end of the line—she's milked the Hawk for his cash and charge-it plastic, then disappeared to resurface three months later broke but with our souvenir of her travels: U.S. Excess bills from here to Hollywooly, which is why we no longer have credit for needs. . . .

But the scorch of the crimson sun in my steaming background takes over my mind. . . . September in Saint Lou means upwards of ninety degrees and the Hawk's refused to invest in an air conditioner, even a hot one sold on the street which we could've picked up for less than fifty bills; but hell, he's in school all day and at work all night, and whitefokes air-condition the whole world in weather like this, their world, or they'd be dropping like flies in this parch, turning to hardline crabs. 'Sides, that's what us darky slaves are for—to work dem fields in dis heat; and we're all over the place in weather like this too, thronged on front porches where it's only ninety degrees, and there's faith in a soon-to-be breeze, come on, *please*. . . .

But picture the Buzzard at the end of our connection, such that it is, with her 170 pounds of solid flesh corralled into royal blue hotpants—she's tossing her wig with its doubledip curls, a faithful facsimile of Sasha Glamouretti's—

"*You heard me,*" she says in response to my pause, and she's waiting in glee. Now see her staging a fainting spell straight from the sell-you-loid screen when she hears news of the Hawk's upcoming marriage to me. (You're having the vapors? But you're cast as faithful Prissy. And see that whitelady over there? Well *she* plays Miss Ann. The Buzzard—she's strictly gone with the wind.)

"You heard me," she says—

"Well now listen," I'm pushed to answer her now with no hint of respect—I mean hell, have I bowed to the sun? In these nine months of pregnancy I've gained forty pounds on a 110-pound frame . . . my chairs are big impossible pillows way down on the out-of-bounds floor . . . and my legs, one leg is swollen to boot, so balloons in the heat with no respect for enough is enough. And Sherlock's getting nowhere (I'm reading *Hound Of the Baskervilles*, last in a series of 1001 Sherlock anthology stories guaranteed to keep you jumping right up to the delivery room)—Sherlock still hasn't solved his case and we've worked all night long on it; his pace must be geared to the heat of Saint Lou, god*damn*—

"Well now listen," I say to the Buzz in sweet dulcet tones; "tell me how you came to convert to this notion" [of chocolate-brown chauvinism]. "Obviously you haven't always felt this way." [Trans. Her Hawkson's my own color, light biscuit-brown—so where'd *he* come from, dropped down from the sky?] And the Buzzard gets it, it takes two to three watson-minutes of her silence for the barb to fade into view, so I'm smiling already by the time it sticks her and she grapples with it. . . . My teeth are like a barricade; sweat runs down my chin in delight. . . . Then there's a faraway click, and the void of her silence.

Next? Through the window I look at the sun.

If you white, you all right. . . . If you yellow, you mellow. . . . If you brown, stick aroun. . . . If you black—get back!

The blackcaste system, reflected from the underside of traditional white-root Dixiemyth hostility, right on up from slavery. Houseniggers vs. fieldniggers, i.e., misedge yellowskin and longstraight hair vs. brown or black skin and the unkinked facsimile. *Bourgie* vs. the pre-bourgeoisie. It's our own blackfokes' inner racism, ricochet racism to call our very own. Our warp. Which's not to say that because I understand the thing, I'm immune.

(But your honors, I'm not yella, not yella, not— well hell, in high school I powdered myself choco- late, Nut Brown to be exact, in days when all blackwomen had to be nutbrown or lump it—dimestore Nut Brown, the time-release cheap formula. By noon I'd have turned burnt orange by way of casual meta- morphosis, due to inferior ingredients in my make-up. Or call it highnoon yella with shades of confusion. But yellaness is relative; it's a state of the soul. Yall hear me?)

Now the Hawk's a skincolor curio in his family— the Bobolinks are all brown to black skinned, and the Hawk sticks out like a sore yella thumb. But among my kin, I blend right in. Between all our yella streaks we've got two red-brown Exceptions. But fuck it, we're black and we've always been black and we took all the cues and we paid all our dues. . . .

FADE TO FLASHBACK: Pale-skinned Great- granma Megloe, for a good case in point, her auburn washboard hair waves notwithstanding, a schoolteacher against the grain and the rest of the odds, she was chastised viciously once, back in the Land of Cotton (*Look away!* You got that right) for hanging out with her own husband, great-grampa Hannibal, who was cinammon-skinned. Greatgranma Megloe was a niggerlovin nigger in disguise. Here's how the story goes across our family reunion table year after year:

PANSHOT: The Attack. Savage whites with their tribal torches one night, sprung up from a primitive ritual somewhere in the rotgut-drunk sacramental backwoods, overalls covered with flapping sheets made of cotton, nigger-picked, invading Megloe turf to punish the "white" woman, Great-granma Megloe and to castrate the "coon," Great-grampa Hannibal. It's three a.m. or so and the marauders are hot with their righteous charge/ad-hoc assignment.

ZOOM IN: Inside the cabin a baby's screaming in terror—it's Grampa Hannibal II as a tot.

TIGHT SHOT: An alien boot clomps on the porch . . . a torch sucks the wood of the roof: *"Hey, nigger! An that white nigger bitchgal too!"*

FREEZE FRAME: From inside the shack comes a shotgun's triplicate boom, and two hoods and one tall white duncehat pop up like firecrackers. (Great-grampa Megloe said his mama didn't name him Hannibal for nothin; if Hannibal-One could prevail with those elephants up in the Alps, he knew he could handle a handfulla crackers in the Dixiemyth woods an tell *his* tale too!) And Great-granma Megloe's busy meanwhile chucking her own torches, dipping coal-oiled firewood into the woodstove and flinging it through the cabin's window-holes at the nightriders outside: *Here, take this shish-kebob!* (Said later her hair was all singed at the edges; she reached up to knot it back into a chignon and it came off in her hands like a wig.) Which's when Ma & Pa Megloe flash-vote to beat it out of Dixiemyth Dodge on the double and they escape North (didn't recognize the contradiction) to Yankeemyth, where bigotry's hoodless and diurnal.

*   *   *

Even so though, despite his responsiveness of sem-
blance of such to Dr. A, the Hawk remained incom-
municado throughout the Xmas season, grudging
through our flat with no visible means of support but
his grumps, til finally he passes me in our narrow
hallway one day and "What's wrong?" I pipe up,
assheavy watson at it still, bound to muck up with
my lethal belief in Solutions. Yet this time—and
here's what makes me remember it now—strange relief and upfront comfort in our oldshoe rhetorical
roles expands from the Hawk's position to the center
of the hall where I stand motionless, ridiculous.

*Above the Hawk's head should be painted a dripping rain
cloud and empty speech ring, and over mine, a bag of "?!'s"
and burned-out light bulb with a fizz instead of a flash. Or
this scene could be set onstage as a broad symbolic animal act
at the famed Saint Brew zoo. See this farce: Upstage a
befuddled monkey looks on and paces . . . scratches his
head in tomfool confusion while a wigged-out hyena
wrapped in dull purple like my jeans of today, limps from
centerstage into the wings, trailing [badtiming], her til.
Heeheeheehee. . . .*

Then I watch the Hawk's heels as he stalks from
the hall after looking at me, then shaking his head
and laughing mysteriously.

"What?" I say, and he chuckles again. "WHAT?" I
repeat with alarm, and he turns with more grin and
no words, just leaves me to paranoid omen of a vague
unsettled type, I know it, can feel it, so try now to
steel for it— I truss myself up now with girder-type
strength, directional beams of support can come later:
this is how I bolster myself or try to, til later that
night when something happens suddenly that over-
loads my stress points.

Nevermind pressure of present repression, I see it today as slo-mo replay: *The Hawk, exploding in a flash of temper to slam me up against the kitchen window, til I choke out an uncle or two from between his fingers twisting flesh of my neck. My sin: Knowing It All ad-infinitum and mortal overtalking. My first impression: that this midnight choke scene's just like bad movies, marred by clumsy overkill, reduntant action for high-pitched talk gone before— ridiculous show after far too much tell, typical of the awkward-with-art: This director's no dreamer, that's for damn sure. . . . But the bashing of my head against pre-shattered glass snaps me back to rueful reality, dig it or not. . . . "All right, all right!"*

But with no regard for enough, the horror went on to wend forward— I took note of a critical outgrowth right here in the journal, though now I recall how it pained me to do it.

WHAT COMES TO PASS NEXT AT MY OWN INSTIGATION is the Rotten Tomato Incident, a picayune episode where i find myself at kitchen counter in process of slicing a dinner salad tomato so as to parcel rotten parts to the Hawk's plate in a clandestinely devilish way— I'm tucking the rot carefully under all's well cover-up salad dressing so the Hawk'll beak it down without a care while i grin in sneaky revenge, an unbelievably little gesture of mine that disgusts me to discover. ("Just don't let anybody take you down to the little level," Double would say; "some folks are so little, they're pathetic!") So when i bust myself i'm filled with disgust at culprit me (Look what you've come to!) caught in felony act, in possession of concealed littleness all while I make out that everything's everything, at least on the surface. Just look at me in would-be revenge; this is so silly, it's fatuous even to me and besides, "Vengeance is mine," saith the Lord. "I'm better equipped to provide it."

It's realizing this that forces me to take a close look at my nature. I'm no sneak attacker and never've been; I've always held it's what's up front that counts to readjust your case. (Frontal attackers always believe this; we use it as a shield to wield in any confrontation til defeat's ensured.) This is why the Hawk's cold front is intolerable: His standoff provokes my blackclash, after which my blackclash provokes his standoff, then here we go round again, time after time, tomato after tomato, regardless of my weary resolution not to lash back but to duck and bear it 'cause somebody's got to give, and I know my cue when I see it. Yet despite that dumb vow, now I face up and dig—even I can dig the impasse of this last-ditch dead-end at least enough to see how while the Hawk trudges toward his goal, I mince along beside him with my journal of hope noting woes and rebuffs, including this note—it's my last before I got hat and decided to duff:

THE HAWK AND I GO TOGETHER LIKE WHITE ON RICE, which is to say we bring out the worst in each other faithfully as each other's half of needed distress, a sickly combination. I see what I'm doing: I drink not to think of our impossibility. . . .

I could see part of it then and I see it all now— It erupts from the depths and it grabs me, my closet ambivalence and consequent guilt. How is it that I couldn't make heads or tails of it before, having only the notion that I had to change to adjust: I was rocking our boat by force of fickle habit which I should stop immediately for everyone's sake—*Just stop it right now!* I slapped myself inside. . . .

What could I do then but walk from the Hawk, regardless of upcoming probable life as a doctor's wife sconced in sumptuous mansion? A mansion's no sanctum from siege against spirit, or so I said then in black-and-white thought before life on my own in this urb of today. . . .

I said then I'd search for personal priorities, and right away set out to do this with monstrous intent, driven by me-search in months after my taking of leave from the Hawk when it seems that no sooner've I flown free from the nest than I'm forced to crash land in a swamp of myself. But— *There's no need to brood on blockage of the past*, I said to my *I*— no need to brood and grow consternated; just lean on your trellis of pith and grow forward . . . grow onward and upward to optimal life in the urb of San Fran!

III

Highrise Construction:
Schemes of the Urb

A System of Transit, a Route
Through the Urb

T he alarmclock goes off and so does my memory. Recollec-
tions stream through my body and out through my eyes—
recall of the pain on this plane, where life resumes with a
roar and a wrench of the soul. With only ringing to warm
me, I'm dragged back to this crack of the cosmos, where I'm
confined in deadly dimensions: the world's brutal judgments.

All I want to know is why I was seen chasing up and
down green hills of my dream, abandoned by the Hawk in a
nameless shack where I wake with a shudder next to a burly
thug—he's got his long twisted dick pressed to my side.
"Baby, just let me put it in" he love-whispers to me, and
inwardly I scream in response to busted cherry of the psyche
. . . while outwardly I simply jump up, dress calmly in the
speed of a flash (damn tight jeans!) and explain that I
would if I could but I can't— ". . . Uh, see, I've got this

*anti-social disease that'll chew your prize to shreds the min-
ute you put it in my near vicinity, an that's the truth so
help me. . . ."*

*Then suddenly I'm running down hills of no-return, up
and down slopes of testimonial torments and triumphs—past,
present, and caustic current of This Is Your Life, you
screwball, even in your dreams, madrapist on your heels for
one element, all of which says what? about your control—
til finally I can't stand it—the therapy of our dreams can be
fatal!—so I wrench myself out of the ether and I freefall
down into waking life, a seizmonaut gone mad enough to
wig all the way back into the world, where I land at the
edge of my Sealedcrest mattress on the floor, with a primal
shriek to greet my neighbors through our paper-mâché terri-
torial apartment wall.* (Ah, another death and rebirth
in the night, *they sigh in their nightfogs, and roll over in
urban-sad sleep.*)

On the bus that first solo morn in San Fran, I'm
one of a hundred folks in the standard aberroe-normoe
mulligan stew. *To Exit, PUSH* says the sign here
beside me, meaning push to get out, or in for that
matter. All these foreigners, racial balancers surrounding emigrant me— They push to get into the hut
built for twenty, push to get up in the morning and
into desperate djellabahs, push against primitive plows
in timewarp drytitty fields of old, push across the sea
to Demomyth where they sway in a pack under the
Statue of Freedom, panicky pushmad mob that they
are, the yearning so-and-soes with caps in hand, these
begging raw dregs of our melting pot who'll push to
mid-peak of our di-gel valhalla. . . .

From my spectator's seat in the rear of the bus I

see a homebred habitant turn to obtrusive alien: "*SAY, Jim! Who you think you pushin, Jack?*"

The Muni #22 is a salvation bus, a veritable liferaft on wheels rescuing warfarers from street hazards of San Fran, even taking emergency refugees who rush up the bussteps right off the top of the moment the door grinds open so that they can latch onto the front busrail lifebar: *Just let me hang onto here for a moment—* It's a bus of victory, the #22 Fillmore, a rolling fuck-you to fearful social separators. Well check it out, today we've got overstuffed dowagers, skoolkid skeptics, attaché case coordinators, secret thermos addicts, deadly desperados, rubbersock bagladies, swinging ferngirls, radioteens, junkies in every shape, size and disguise, straights, gays, wavies and spirals like yourself, you name em. The muni and her muniacs! Why, this muni coach could be any ghetto-to-glory transit vehicle swaying from deathtrap valley to mansion heights, clamped to an overhead cable for protection of her passengers, so as not to wing right off into outer space at one of her points of transition. At midhill Pacific Street maybe, where street thugs turn into lil olelady wrinklers with their paranoia and pocketbooks.

Five, four, three, two. . . .

As we cough up to the crest of the slope where Malcatraz lurks into view, I slice the bus in cross-section with my mind's blade and I peel her laterally, which is when I can make out our wide-angle hodge-podge, rows of human pinheads blurring together, standing/sitting side by side. I focus on one wrapped in toast-tone skin, her eyes two craters: a tight shot, where I zoom into mundane day-to-day me, on the way to the Illfare Department for my soon-to-be monthly AFDC. Through the window beside me I'm able to see isolated buildings pop into view all over the urbscape below me, most of them in the City Center with its upward lush life on one side, and downhill crush life on the other—a sidelit scene which shapes into sight as sleepy sunshine flickers on her spotlights one by careful one.

Another building's lit even as I note this, the Dole Office, situated in an overstated setting of bandit territory visible in the valley below as the bus chugs downward toward the Skirt Steak District with passengers shooting wish-energy at maximum force: *Just get us away from these slums!* (Slums, slums, dirty brute word that it is. . . . We prefer the graceful "ghetto.") Walking down these streets is a death-defying act. Streets of grey held-up hope and sodden faith settled by stretch-bandage women in woolen permanent dresses. Scene of garbage grazers, winewashed amputees, sidewalk sitters, gutter sprawlers, street spitters, wall pissers, red-eyed see-all neighborhood watchmen on every corner: *Hey, Mama!* Home of straggling school kids with beknapped kinks and stringing towhair and chopped orient rice bowl cuts, bowlegged, scar-armed, swollen-eyed. . . . Zone of street strutters, pimps and hardcore johns, belly-drag reliefless women. . . . Hey you! Outlaws of the badlands with your brash scenic blunders— What's the taste of your vice when the fog gulps it down?

Projecting stunted vision into risky reality, I see my current confusion in the face of every denizen on this deadend drag. Images of my inner lens. Likenesses of my leery spirit.

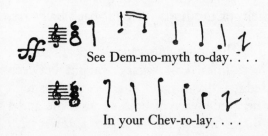

See Dem-mo-myth to-day. . . .

In your Chev-ro-lay. . . .

I dare you to roll down the window. The urban blues should be painted red to match the terror of its lyrics.

Awww . . . Fuck! Nasty sounds and sloppy screws in transient two-buck alleyways/shoot-up passageways— I live in the urb and I've had it! I live in the urb and I could spout bitter barroom blues/could spit sourdough San Spancisco nausea clots to twist your gut into shapes sophisticated sensibility (Well, you'll have these types in any civilization, shrug)—into shapes sophistication needs a psychphylactic for. My feelers are spent shells from citynights tuning into/ turning to anti-toxin Bitches Brew (na dat na dat na datum natum um wat wahhh). . . . A trumpet solo— My whipped-down soul's a trumpet solo, in the fog, on a SF Bay getaway ferry fending for itself in relentless tidal froth!

But who am I fooling with my focus on outside despair? Charity begins at home, and people in houses of panic shouldn't throw stones. I should narrow my scope, face my own closest demon with no more ado or distracting preview. The issue is this: *Can I count on me or not to be solely responsible for me and baby LC?* My heart starts to pump like a piston the moment I pose that query— I picture me sliding into slack-mouthed defeat with LC uncared for, unkempt of spirit, never to know undaunted dawns of new hope.

What's the use? What's the name of this war? It's all I can do to reach for my bottle of fight-back ballistics, my beer. . . .

It's then that the following vision appears to me, when I'm freeze-framed in vagary, caught between fuzzy full-fledged dream and razor-consciousness. Gradually I become aware of bold eyes on me and I flinch, then shrug *Grow up, don't be scared; this is what solo flight feels like, full of spooky vibes and phantom phobia.* . . . In this way a few seconds pass as I look down at my bag of receipts and remnants of myself in the form of i.d.'s for AFDC, collecting courage to confront the wraith that plagues me, finally building to "Hell, I'll reckon with anydamnthing 'fore I let it creep up and take me unarmed!" Then's when I spin around to confront the enemy and find on the bus seat behind me an old woman who favors Great-granma Rose Megloe remarkably—she's the same sturdy-thin with beige pale skin that makes you look again for blunt facial details of saharan giveaway—Yep, she's black—even wears a look-alike chignon and wire-rimmed glasses framing deep savant eyes that beam across granite cheekbones into my slopped-over soul. I blink once. . . . She seems to wink—

Now I'm pushed even more to maintain my neck-crane position so as to investigate further, but I'm held back by penalizing politeness of my upbringing: *Don't stare.* (But I'm not finished looking!) Yet with old folks you should have respect until proven otherwise, so I'm suffused by a wave of crashing ambivalence when I hear or feel these words splash into my syzygy. . . .

Fool, don't you see that the theory of relativity— Look at

118

that. No sooner than I say "relativity," Einstein crosses your mind. Ignorant! Relativity is a concept invented and sustained by Strong Black Women! Einstein in his laboratory overseas just brought up the rear of the discovery, and in theory at that. Don't you see? Our Theory of Relativity is what you could call the hand-me-down remedy for all kinds of historic despair, including your delusion of loss of bearings on an uncharted course. Why wait to see which way the wind blows? Follow your nose to your backbone! Take a lesson from your gone-befores!

Now as much as I hate to admit to the matriarch, that advice is just what I need to hear, wobbly me, wilting at the touch of new soil with lioness root disregarded in its trail through my past; assuming that wisdom gained from past deeds is what's meant by "gone-befores," and this is what I make of it. Consequently, I run down a list of fleshed-out gone-befores in my memory, while their blood's still warm— but strange, there must be more to mayhem control than self-centered conjecture; what's one isolate trek to ownself redemption? I brood about this, my unseemly singular solitude, to such an extent that I realize, *The one is the many, and the many are the one.* It's then that I'm seared by the eyes behind me and called forward to the edge of my seat. . . . Then with no further preview I'm snatched out of my head into a gust of my matriarch's vision, with its timetorn images along the road to today, seeing this cinema with my soul blanched white as the screen:

Ruptured guts—
                    packhorse cottongin breeding women w/
warped spines & ruptured guts . . . mothers of 16 children,

6 alive. . . . Wives of tobacco/cotton/stovewood/spinning wheels/ragdiapers/magic menus/miracle potions for the damn-near dead. Mothers of mortgaged children. Calamity handlers. Tragedy tamers. Survivor-resisters against the odds & versus all bets, in spite of/afterall/nevertheless/ regardless— longshot ancestresses, ferrous-willed women flying through the eye of the scourge. Dark phoenixes in a far-fetched flock, with wings that sing RISE

with us!

The bus is scaling the crest of a slope with her coach full of folks poised in unified ho-hum stare and newspaper trance as I sit here, riding waves of yesteryear til I hear a snatch of dialog beside me that makes me sit up and take note.

"Well, what really concerned *me*," says one slammed commuter to another (young plain brown-attached government work-woman to shine-coiffed, lip-glossy corporate successette); "was I knew I had to leave him in order to grow into a more developed space"—a consideration that nudges me in the ribs of my brain *vis á vis* Charlie the Hawk, just what I need now, thoughts of ex-husbandly Charlie—but that's how the blues requires you to slide down a list of your barbs one by one to cues all around. . . . *In order to grow into a more developed space*— Me too! I want to shout and tug this talker's coattail, at least for the while, when I'm still convinced of camaraderie. But there's something dividing us, a key distinguishing factor. . . . I left Charlie due to looming dead end up ahead, so I made my move by default in a way, by non-assertive, no-choice default; I didn't even split in a way, I just refused to go further.

From the first the Hawk was actually independent and needing no one, so he said— He'd accomplish what there was to do and needed no one by his side to pull it off or bluff it thru. "You only have yourself," he said and neatly lived this, lives it now, will live it yet, nevermind the arrival of me on his scene seriously believing No man is an island. . . . *I sailed up to his turf on my raft, shared my ration with him anyway (forcefed it when necessary), left my hopping footprints in his secluded sand. . . .*

(Ah, but you split for green pastures you thought, or greener grass at your detour. Remember the green you could see in the distance?)

No, frankly I don't or I won't, and why should I whip myself with that dream while I'm here in this dearth? Look here, so I've touched down alone for a moment with my resource parachute still unfurled, made an ass-heavy landing out here in urban swamp where it's the best I can do to hold baby Mia up over my head, just keep her high and dry by any means available, by life-preserving welfare even—it's not an airtight resource; it makes for a raggedy float, but welfare'll move us forward one piddling lap at a time as long as it knows it's not our only option for survival. A few minutes from now I'll submit my life data and bingo! my number's in the bureau-hat; my case comes to pass in three weeks. I'll be a freshman welfare drawee, first in the family to go on the dole. Hey Ma, look at me. . . . What would Muz say if she knew? Or Double, my dad, for that matter?

Muz has such disdain for AFDC, tracing from past social work days when she was dutiful skip tracer of fathers-on-the-lam at a time when welfare homes were required by law to be fatherless, in olden days eight years ago. Muz would bounty hunt for fathers who were sneaking to live at home; but from grinding commitment to permanent bonding of the family unit if possible, when she came upon job-hunting fathers living at home she'd look the other way, Muz said—"I trace them, then I skip them. . . ." Yet Muz is a great depression grad from a family with no welfare scars among them, kin to a miracle— The Megloes didn't believe in the dole and never touched it through growth and development of six kids, even under one-blouse circumstances like young Muz's (then called "Vole") during her up-growing years at Stowe Teachers College.

Now as for Double, his mother once touched down on AFDC, taking a piddling dole from a small town in Panhandle Province that meted out one of the sparsest relief benefit amounts in the country; so Double knew welfare blues from inside and had vowed never to repeat-perform them in any way, shape, or form, from any angle, which was partly the cause of his youthful escape from the Panhandle state to Saint Lou of his vigorous dreams.

It's later that day when I'm on the way from my wars at welfare thinking, Now it's all on me, the burden of proof of potential for basic breadwinning, take-it-to-the-bank breadwinning on a day-in, day-out basis. One thing Charlie did without flaw or fuck-up was Good Providing, which he insisted on doing completely on his own and I never even thanked him for it, at least not with words or special respect; I just didn't realize—Damn! How did we feel to him, Mia and I, riding his plans with our spurs of dependence? Likely heavy as unwieldy lead, and he never made a squawk of balking at his frisky burden. What's worse, *Why should he?* I thought at the time. He can handle it; he's the *man*, so my thinking went. . . .

I can't help but brood about this, gnash it to bits in my mind as I'm headed to pick up Mia from her kindergarten via Muni #6 wending through San Fran's Hashberry District, a place where you take a life curriculum condensed into an intensive seminar whenever you enter its neighborhood gates. A pink-haired boy with his rusted meathook, a spike-headed girl with hair like crippled sunshine—she clutches a doll with hat pins in its deflated chest— Street urchins are folding momentary sleeping bags under weary eucalyptus trees as far as the eye can see. The scene, with its multicolored rags and tatters, is a patchwork quilt in motion, a fabric scheme we weave beyond so that now I can see Mia's and my Vista Valley homestead set in panoramic relief way down below. When I squint and shade my eyes I can even make out the house where we live, a clean, first-impressive mansionoid building which we live in one room of with baleful bars on our windows, so much for illusions of busy hi-classhood that permeates this part of the neighborhood surrounding Diablo Square, our scene hilltop community park where parkgoers come in two shifts: on-edge diligent daygoers and uh-oh, watch it! twist-minded nightgoers. . . .

Of the four blocks surrounding the Square, one of them is the postcard/calendar/movie/t.v. "Streets of San Span" favorite on-location street, home of old money real-estate speculators and dope-baron, new money reality owners. . . . Another is Mia's and my constant traffic, screechbrake, clang-bell muni trolley-running street, while a third street is the neighborhood primary siren street of traditional criminal getaways—this street of round-the-clock cop and ambulance sirens has synchronized traffic lights and plenty of vacant lots and condominia under construction, so's an expedient throughfare to anything at all; and a fourth street is home of a huge-antic drop-outs' high school named Opportunity High where kids in trouble, on trouble, of trouble are dumped and clumped together in a crisis-oriented course of study, never-mind planning and logic aforethought.

As for our monoroom apartment in that maze of the urb, each of us has a corner of the room that belongs only to that one of us. I have my corner containing my throne and combination hassock-table, the throne being an overstuffed recycled recliner that's heavenly in all but appearance; Mia has her corner full of toychest and toys like her thousand tiny-piece Erecto erector set the object of which is to dispense, disperse, and scatter mini-components throughout one's pre-school household in places that require a small child's devilish dispatch to devise— A small round red piece with raised plastic pustules was found in a cake that I baked, my rear molar found it late one sleepless night two weeks ago, so Mia's restricted "corner" for her belongings is a thing of theory really; and PrimeTime, our found cat who moved in with us after we'd fed him for three weeks in a row and we'd treated his wounds from canine mugging in the Square across the street— PrimeTime has his corner containing his litter box, which he sniffs and rejects, and his dishes of leftovers and water, which he sniffs and suspects. At any rate, the fourth and final corner's our kitchen strip of stove and fridge next to the front door with its side window look-out, through bars of rust, onto the San Fran view of flash-assembled downtown highrises, as orderly as if they'd been spat or spitted out from between a giant's teeth except for the hulking unique-shapen Spansamerica pyramid sticking out and up all on its individual own, a tower of strange, unexpected and seeming silly strength saying, *Just look at me in my irregularity. Now ain't this just like San Spancisco?*

The bus is moving midhill now, scaling the crest of the slope with the speed of a snail, weary engine churning with effort of stressful pull, brakes screaming as we slip backward two feet for each foot forward in our gas pains, fume indigestion, lower back blockage of passengers silent-shifting in vehicle bowels. . . . In the movement I can see my own chugging individual journey, through a fog of incomprehension that lifts when I least expect it, like the heartless haze of San Fran, sporadic, universal, relentless. But what's this I hear from the busstranger beside me (an older, motherly Sister, with back-to-basics nod of Hello to me as I look and smile, then look away just to listen). . . .

"Life style? What's a 'life style'? In my day—Honey, when they talk about livin, these kids nowdays sound like they flippin through a wallpaper catalog!"

That's right, nods a heavy-set woman seated in front of her.

"Life's what you make it. And I mean from skid
row to Pacific Peaks!"

"*Say* it."

"You take it from the git-go, just as it is."

"Make it *plain*."

"Back in the old days, in them shacks down there
in the Bottom, they didn't waste much time choosin
they *life*style—"

"Sho' you right."

"What they *did* was trim the devil outa the bag
they found theyself tucked down into though."

"Make *do*. Girl, you ain't said nothin but a word!"

That's it, that's my cue—just make do, say fuck-
you to rue at this stage of my life, this is just a phase
I'll zing through and turn back later to smile at or nod
at at least; this is just my time out or break time. We
all get booked for break time sometimes—our clock
gets stopped from the outside, so what's there to do
but just use this break to good advantage, face up to
my fouls in the past and game-plan my moves coming
up. . . .

"The Spirit assigns you consecutive lessons to teach
what you need to learn in this life," dear daddy
Double said to me once. "And that's the point of our
pain: it gets our attention and causes us to keep our
eye on the blackboard of hope in order to figure it
out. Yet, wouldn't you know it? Sometimes still we
fail to keep focus so that we flunk the next test which
makes us have to be held back, to repeat the same
lesson again and again when all we want is to gradu-
ate finally, so we can move on out into life up ahead!"

But what's this commotion up front in the bus,

with busdriver shouting to quick-entering passenger, *"Hey, young man, get up offa that quarter! This ain't no hitch-hike!"* And he pauses, braced for return lip/ commentary, which boomerangs back down the aisle in no time flat.

"What's it to you? You workin on commission, Blood?"

The voice of bus passenger issues from a man walking toward me on his way to the steerage compartment in the back of the bus. *"Hey, sweet thing!"* he says as he passes me and I see that uh-oh, it's Kwame Ochudareshi walking backward, back up the bus aisle toward me as if by vibe, Kwame of Reality Rap Restaurant, neighborhood enterprise sponsored by doomed Reality Rap Halfway House for ex-convicts— Kwame with his open mouth of amazing minute-to-minute observations, with hand outstretched in power salute-greeting, multicolored woven *kufani* askew on the side of his head, shoulder bag stuffed with *Strategy For A Black Agenda, Africa Must Unite,* etc., along with plastic bag of mysterious relaxation implements, outlawed stress-release paraphernalia.

His raffi sandles flap in haste to the suddenly vacated seat at my side as he says, *"Hey, Mama, check this out. Now listen good, you hear?"* (This he shouts til heads turn.) *"Good, I'm glad you're hearing me, nobody really— You got to be on your toes every minute, see—"* (With this last he lays a veiny fist on my knee and leans close to share his winebreath)—

"See? Every goddamn minute you got to be on your. . . . The Man'll sneak attack if you don't! He'll sneak attack and ain't we all hip now! I mean all ages, sizes, an shapes of us! This is a TRUTH, baby, but folks don't wanna hear it!

"*Got to brace yourself though; it'll scratch you some on the way down, the truth always does, so most folks back off terrorized, hear me? but not you and hell, not these old sisters RIGHT HERE!*" (He leans forward to tap the seatback of the two old blackwomen sitting in front of us, so close to me now that I see the dark tinge of his inner nostrils, burned by self-inflicted arson of firepowder, consciousness-remover to clear passages to new world of mock freedom. Uh-oh, he's enslaved again.)

"*Ha. My highschool counselor— Did I ever tell you my highschool counselor advised me to go into cabinetmaking, the motherfucker, and I said 'Man, don't you know there's some dialectical material in my future that necessitates HIGHER LEARNING, which is definitely in my master plan. Now just show me how to get there, that's all you can do for me! That, and shut your career placement book for the rest of your life. . . .'*

"*Fact is, under the circumstances, I mean with all this jive you go through out here in this farce, I SHOULD'VE been a cabinetmaker, but shit, that's when I enrolled in the street academy, my own personal street academy. FUCK a cabinet!*

"*Check them out.*" (He leans closer to the old women up ahead and cocks an ear with his head almost in my lap so that I see the pulsing network of veins that bulge in and out near his eye. He grabs my knee: "*Listen!*"

". . . and my baby boy," one old woman's in process of saying, "well, he just graduated from State University down there in L.A.— He says, 'Mom, I'm so disgusted. I looked an I walked til my feet were sore, an I ain't got a thing to show for it.' See?

Now *that's* the reason I keep tryin to prepare him for the roughness out here—"

"Uh huh," says her friend. "Well I always tell mine, To get a good job, you gotta know somebody that *knows* somebody."

"I could have *got* him a job, but I want him to know it ain't easy—"

"Quiet as it's kept—"

"—cause Mama might won't be around all the time—"

"It's a cryin shame. Kids go through four, five years of school nowadays an can't even get a job out here, even in the post office like it used to be for some of us—"

"Not in *no*body's office."

"I'm here to tell you! An my daughter, she been lookin for somethin so long, she started losin heart. I told her, Don't you forget: You might be down, but you ain't *out*!"

"Thass right."

"So she say, 'Mama, I know what I'm go do— Maybe I'll volunteer then.' "

"Aw yeah?"

"An I told her, 'Well go on an volunteer then, keep yourself busy. Do *some*body some good with your free time—' "

"You told her right."

"*See?!*" Kwame cuts in with a cry and reaches to squeeze one woman's shoulder in comrade-elation, causing movement all around us, reflex jumps of alertness: Uh-oh, he's getting physical. . . . "*See!*" Kwame shouts, "*Now here's two Sisters who can dig a young man like me, with a— Yeah, yall hear me too!*" (He gestures with sweeping hand motion to include onlookers)—*"That's right, I'll tell the world!"* He turns to the placid-buddha blackwomen whose eyes focus through spectacles on vibrating Kwame. Thinking she's undetected, one nudges the other: Now what do you think of this?

"That's right," Kwame repeats to his target, *"I'll tell the world: I had a job, a hustle, and a paper route, and they ALL got pulled! I HATE this place. It's a town where they'll give a job to a goddamn ESKIMO or* (Here he pauses to look in the aisle beside at a gay flincher who's wishing he could tuck in his leather chaps and just disappear) *"—or to a do-funny sissy,"* says Kwame—

"But not to us!" This booms suddenly from a tall wild-mannered man approaching over feet and bags in the aisle, banging shoulders of people looking away in self-defense as the bus pulls up to its stop.

" 'Us,' hell, *motherfucker!"* Kwame shouts in anti-welcome to his would-be partner. *"You— I don't know you but I know you 'cause I see you, in the looking glass of death!"* (He stops for a moment to laugh with a bray.) *"Answer me this!"* he screams as the interloper panic-muscles his way to the front. *"Why is there dancing in the slave quarters?"* And with that, Kwame folds a protective arm around the pouch of his bag and sprints to the rear door and out. . . .

"Call me!" he shouts to my window as the bus pulls away. *"I'm at the Cadillac Hotel on Leavenworth Street. Call me! Call me!"*

In aftermath silence my thoughts come shuffled out of sequence, this ace first: I met Kwame last month, at a time when I'd managed to scrape enough bread to send Mia to the sitter for the night, a sitter who was recommended by the cook at her soon-to-be preschool, and from nothing to do and knowing nobody I'd wandered through the neighborhood after the evening's meditation on my break from Charlie thinking, At any rate, I've made my break while the gettin's as good as it's gonna get; I've made my split for salvation, so now I have to lie with it; which brings to mind how I can't imagine going onward through the days without Charlie's body next to mine through transfusion nights. . . . Instead I feel bleak stretching silence of our separation, see stranger's lips smiling then sucking my Charlie, licking and lapping, laughing, wink—scenes that could snap me right back to my cage of caged feeling for Charlie, though in the glare of flashing red inside my head I could see that we were no good for each other, Charlie and me—we gave each other far more pain than pleasure. . . . What's more, Charlie was developing straight ahead from our hook-up but wait, Hey! wait up for me. It was like Double said, "You never stand still in this life; whether you know it or not you're either moving forward or backward." And there's no doubt about it, any fool can see that I'm in reverse and out of control, drifting backward, downward, and off to the side, feeling so hollow and empty inside, mired in sadness of deadly inertia, love-needy me, used-to-be whining to Charlie in so many ways:

I need to be loved! I just want your support!

"Well people in hell, they want ice water," Charlie would say, shrugging me off with a grin. Suddenly then I could see that Charlie would never nurture me; he had no tits and hole for stockpiling passionate payback to earth for our birth in the way that women

come equipped to do our own regeneration, right on the premises. ("Muz," I thought, "you could've taught me that; I ought to know better than to look for my man to be my mother! And Double, what's your excuse? Just look at how you raised me, weak with clumsy expectations and ingrown hope of grown via the vine that I'm tacked to at the time, too blind to see that Charlie's an emotional miser, he clamped down on love long ago as a kid of his love-stingy home." Long before I skipped down his briarpath, Charlie was unavailable for relationship, he was never at home when love-company called, so how could he come to the door of his heart?

Brooding on this I'd wandered through the neighborhood on the night that I first met Kwame, stopping at bars til in no time I'm boozed with head bad enough to forget how it is that I wind up at home, when it's due to Kwame who's taken it upon himself to walk me home and then to fade away with nervous chivalry.

But in the new apartment, my mind's being pronged back and forth between alternate demons including one, the ghost of sadness present, who insists on self-focus, that weird hocus-pocus that causes me to fire on myself with a fusillade of desperate questions, like *How do you look at three* A.M. *at home behind your barricade?* From fear and rattling What Else I've barricaded myself in for the rest of Saturday nite, til I get the urge to wend my way upstairs and knock on my neighbor's door— He's Prince Charming; I'm the damsel dressed in overstress.

Which fiends have come to the fore in my face? (Face of twisted bulldog jaws in my green bentonite beauty masque, with hair standing locked in dread maze of plaits.) They all want to come out at once!, my grabbag of ghouls, jamming their barrier one at a time til one sneak-squeezes through while I'm too wasted to realize. I'm too busy weaving upstairs, now poised in nitegown outside new neighbor's door, where from depths inside I hear female giggles trill over peaceful mood music of pleasure-night, George Winsome's sensuous singing, . . . *before fools and kings . . . the greatest thing you could ever learn . . . is to love . . . and be loved . . . in return. . . .*

Our song! Or so it seems at the time—mine and, and whose? But already I've rung the bell and my answer's on his way to the door when an under-ground ghoul sets me up then hops out, Bang! for all to see while we wait; it's me as defeatee sinking away from the surface, disgusting drowning underdog, sickening— It's useless, I can't swim this course: I lash myself with this on my way through the waves, seasick, repugnant. . . .

But here he is now, my saving prince. How long? Nothing to say. Just the hang of his face like a brown-shoe moon suspended in the open doorway, repelled in soft focus, frowning me away from his heretofore threshold.

It was March, just last month, when I left; I re-member the spring back to life of the streets—the Hashberry District on bus-windowed mornings or riding with Mia through Golden Grail Park with its bands of urban gypsies camping on the green. *Spring, Spring, it don't mean a thing; it exhausts me, excludes me as far as I can see*— All I could see was my personal great depression, a cavity filled with decay and no growth, so to raise out of myself I'd listen for hope in the sound of the voices around me each busday.

"He THINKS he knows. I said to him, 'Boy, you don't know nothin but what somebody TOLE you. You done read about life, or heard about it. I've LIVED my life. I know what life's all about."

"Now I can dig THAT."

"You hear me? I'll snatch him offa that thousand-dollar racin' bike an break his pale pink neck. An I'm not even violent! I don't have to be. I've THIS, up here, these smarts in my head! He's scared-a me not becaws of what I am, who I am—he's down on me 'caws of his fancies about me, what's already in his mind about me!"

Amazing, the mechanics of may-be-soon mayhem brought to pass by misunderstanding, mayhem premeditated, yet unplanned as a stock resort— It fascinated me, the whole psychology of *be prepared*, just in case (to the point of what would be called "paranoia" under any other circumstances but dusky life in Demomyth). *Be prepared*, that whole psychology, it causes me to reappraise my rationale for splitting from Charlie in light of new evidence just heard from a stranger on the bus because like the brother talking, Charlie's inclined to raw rage, but he keeps it tucked inside due to probable upbringing by his mother, the Buzzard, her threats of *"Be good! Don't be so mannish!"* at a time when he's kneehigh to a duck, still young and impressionable—the Buzzard having hooked up with a gambler who'd gotten his hat right before the Hawk was born, never to return to the scene of his crime, yielding *All men are rotten* in the Buzz book of cut and dry blight. Charlie must have heard that

synopsis a trillion times, he was forcefed that lesson
through the tit, took in bitters with his breast milk,
so how could he be but constipated in his love for
himself and for me, and now for young Mia?

I should understand this and I do, in theory at
least, but not enough to insist on acting out compas-
sion, I'll admit it— I can feel myself resist further
understanding in order to steel against corrosion of
my original resolve at a time when I've already exam-
ined the issues and fomented my fadeaway from Charlie. Wobbling back and forth on the fence to my
freedom could maim me or cleave me, or cause me to
lose focus from looking at all at once, til everything
blurs. Multi-path distortion can be fatal to your plans!
Besides, I can't help him— Charlie's too embittered to
celebrate blessings like his freedom so far from constant death pending by way of arbitrary sentence to
prison, cop attack by mistake or misthought, or false
refuge dope and street crime—curses I knew or saw
or learned about from Double—curses that claimed
so many neighborhood boys who were here one day
and gone the next, to black boys' happy living grounds
in the phase after death, where they could live out
the rest of their lives in peace, away from earthly
target duty. Somehow Charlie was blessed in his
growing up years—saved from the plague, the door
of his youth was passed over.

"The black male is an endangered species," Double used
to say; yet I couldn't make use of that crippling
composite to justify my life with Charlie ("the Hawk"
as I called him back then)— Compensation's one theme,
not my themesong in life. I had to be me-first and

name my own tune; had to name that tune soon, before I grew to be tone deaf for good.

"I was all messed up, just like you," says a tired voice beside me, and looking I see a thin tan-skinned woman with sad wincing eyes of fed-up surprise—she's talking to a partner in time who comprehends the overall scheme of her victimized crime. "When I left Q," she continues, "I felt so free, away from that clamp-down—"

"Later for *that*," proffers her friend.

"But the killin thing is, when I was leavin, I caught myself tryin to lighten up an old gravity-ass. 'It's all my fault,' I said—"

"Say *what?*"

"There I was, tryin to ease up on him, after all his stunts too—the hot-air ego, the rip-off routine, the pink pussy complex, his non-stop lies—him runnin the *game*, as long as your leg—"

"Go 'head an say it."

"Blood even grew some dreads and started wanting me to tip along ten paces behind him, accordin to the Old Testament, he said—"

"Be for real."

"—not ten paces, ten centuries back to our place in the veil. You know, with the baby on our back, cut off *thing* so we can't feel no pleasure, and trippy long skirts, like in 'All right now, Woman Number Two. Bring me my peanut stew!' "

"What you say!"

"That's when I realized—"

"You got wise."

"I got a weak heart and a weak stomach too."

"Honey, I hear you!"

"I *hate* long goodbyes; o.d. *quick* from a heavy load of shame-on-you! So when he starts goin off on me the day that I'm leavin', I sez to him, 'Look. Let's keep this thing down to a low roar, ok? No reasons, excuses, or lies are necessary at this funeral.' "

She sounds so sure of herself, enviably so; all surety is enviable to me in my violent vacillation— I'm still considering her calm, or was it fatigue? and the way that as she spoke she reached down to yank her idling toddler so that his feet barely touched the floor of the bus with no show of emotion on his part or hers— he's used to it; is she? I can't help but slide into reverie, picturing me with Mia, jejune chickadee, in the time of terror we shared just a few, it was two, months ago.

On the day of the dog attack Mia and I had been walking all over San Fran, combing the unfamiliar urb for an apartment. "It's all my fault," I thought; "sooner or later I'll learn how to *plan*. It's in this fashion of fatigue and ingrown anger that I stumble into the yard of an advertised rental address, past a small warning sign that says what?—Who cares? I'm weary to the point of no respect for hand-lettered signs of opinion, just leading peevish sleepy Mia. "Just one more look and we'll be on our way," I say to the Chick as I close the gate behind us and take two or three steps forward—Mia's beside me now, when I hear a low, close growl up ahead and feel terror reflex instantly. . . . No time to think, I just feel myself snatch Mia's hand and draw her close to my legs, warning "Wait! Just stand still!" as I wrench a look toward tall grass parting in narrowing distance to reveal a squat albino pitbull padding toward us with teeth bared beneath confident red-rimmed eyes. . . .

A scream— Mia starts in low register, cooking up by degrees to high pitch, and the dog moves forward a pace, taking his time— *"Shhh! I need you to help me,"* I say, but Mia's response is to stiffen in shock when I squeeze her scared sparrow hand.

"Get behind me," I tell her— "Now move with me wherever I go. I might have to let go of your hand—" and with that Mia snatches her hand from mine, she misunderstands. I feel my shoulder bag sag with her weight as the Chick jumps behind me with a whimper; she's clinging to the straps of the bag. . . . Then I see the dog move forward one more step, he stands apace in temporal space, still for a moment with front paws braced in a back-leaning slant. My eyes scan the yard and take note of a stick; it seems to be thick, and it's only a few meters away. . . .

Mia, be with me— With one arm behind me I cup her up close to my spine, but as soon as we move, the dog growls and he poises to lunge. *At last I could give. Say goodbye to this strife of stick-to-itude. Just follow my nose to the gel of my backbone.* But then

"STAY!" says a firm voice that I recognize as mine; I've come to realize suddenly that watchdogs must be trained so responsive to order; therefore be firm, first with him, then with me— *Just get to the stick and then chop through his throat.* . . . No time to waste focus on disabling fear, but the dog seems to hear my resolve, here he comes. . . . I dangle my purse in his sight and leap for the stick with Mia still clinging, adhesive, she's light as a feather with her scream like a roar—

138

Then "BLANCO! Get back!" comes a shout from afar, from a pale-eyed man on a porch that materializes apparition-like into load-filled cognition. (Where were you and your porch all along?) And the dog turns reluctantly to trot toward its master who narrows his eyes at me and yells, "How dumb can you be! Didn't you see the sign?"

WATCH YOUR STEP! says the bus sign beside me. WATCH YOUR HEAD, it should read; YOUR FEET HAVE EVOLVED TO A POINT OF SELF-SUFFICIENCY. . . . What I need is to heed all such signs of my times and my crimes or ruthless good intention, signs that are straight up and clear, posed in fearless, frank language—need to read them in depth at my leisure, starting here and right now on this slow bus to nowhere creeping at crustacean's pace through must be all there is of San Spancisco, from Sunrise District out by the ocean down to last horizon Trappers' Point near Laserbeam Park. Through the window I see a funnel of fog wafting away from the bay, peaceful, serene as it drifts through its duties with a mellow spray of mild rain, and I'm struck by the contrast of this strange new climate to wild rampage thunderstorming hometown Saint Lou with its severed sky of lightning cracks and doomsday tornadoes touching down to terrorize. . . . It's so sedate in San Fran—

"Wooo! Wait! *Stop!*" says a big-wigged woman lurching down the aisle in my direction. "Whoops!" she says to beg pardon of two ogling pacific islanders whose bodies were in the way of her tipsy trail, this being their only sin before their penance in progress:

they'll be circumstantial conversation objects from here on out; this drunk needs a target.

"Ooh, ooh honey, I'm sorry," she says to both as one; "I can't stand to stand still! I didn't mean— Did I step on your foot? Cute little sandals— Look at your toes! I'm— Trouble with me is once I get started, I just don't know how to stop!"

"Me neither!" This last is hurled by an alkie comrade in the rear of the bus near me, a munitizen from the looks of him—he rides one bus after another all day and all night, resides on the public transit system, maybe makes a living here. . . .

"But I'll tell you one thing," says Ms. Wig as she pushes her girth through the crowd toward her feedback in the back. "If I do something wrong, I know how to step forward behind it. Not backward, forward!"

Me too! in my fumbling way— I grunt this aloud to myself and then cough surreptitiously so as to seem normal tucked-in undisturbed while going on to thin. Just don't scrutinize the past if it stings you; that's right, let's forget not regret, it's no sweat as you'll see! I insist that to me as meanwhile the bus groan-hauls toward the crest of hilly Heavenworth Street with its milling out-of-workers, until scree! Metal clangs on metal somewhere under back bus wheels. . . . Then there's heat rising to the soles of my feet, to my legs, to my seat; and rear engine co-passengers start to seek out each others' eyes, reluctantly: *Now what is this crap?* as out time-worn hillmobile sighs down to a heave so that we almost come to a stop but for collective wish-thrust pushing us up toward flat ground less than five yards away. *Hold that clutch!* And ho!

We pull the peak at a slowpoke's pace only to grind to
a halllt afterall at a familiar fork: twisted Allen Overpass on one side and fat congested Loyce Boulevard
on the other. It's during this interval, when time
seems suspended on the cusp of consciousness, that I
feel myself waft into an earlier dream of a time shortly
after I came to be here on my own in the urb of San
Fran. . . .

*In my dream there's an elevator, & I'm inside with Muz
& the Hawk who's nondescript, his face is gone: just the
impression of seething black in a sweatshirt. The elevator's
old wood, bumping & knocking & dragging along til we
stop by general consensus to let anyone out who chooses to
leave, when suddenly it comes to mind, all of ours at once,
that the way to whip the damn thing into motion's thru an
applied UP!, concerted group effort which we apply at
once. . . . The elevator's rising now more & more quickly
due to group force, so I turn to my tripmates, about to
explain the process of heightened optimism, and that kneedeep
optimism = magic: you can walk on nails / eat fire / pay
your bills / say fuck you to the fed—anydamnthing. And for
proof, I decide to go UP! by myself, right on up past the
shaft into wide open air, up into clouds where I'm floating/
drifting thru blue mesh & white fluffballs/johnson&johnson
vapor. The earth's down below, green & safe from this
angle. . . . I dot in a contented cow or two to round out
the countryside, & I'm smiling & humming—high as I can
be, while as I drift, a lot comes to light. The realization
that once I let up on the vibe, I can expect to descend in
direct proportion to the lapse in my juice. And once, in the
midst of a greeting to earthbound earthlings, I almost touch
down from carelessness. Got to keep an eye on— I could fool*

around & lose my cue like slipshod cinderella; and it's back in the pumpkin again, goddamn! Or I could lose my focus & forget to fly. :Fuckedup priorities. Which is why I bring the thing up again all by myself thru a deep breath of the mind, bearing down in my head like the all-alone strong-woman in the heart of the circus— And whee! Up into clouds again, thanx to just me. Up&away, and hopefully so!

"Hell, the driver oughta have sense enough to detour onto Loyce," says a briefcase bearer in the front of the bus; he knows his calling, so responds instantly to any cue for authority— "He should radio in for a replacement vehicle, there's no other choice." *Am I right?* he stares to two women nearby who snap to intuited duty with reflex agreement; they know their cue too as do nearby busriders nodding and prodding in the headmost bus section:

". . . buses—must be the first models they put on the road. . . ."

"Well if the drivers could *drive*, maybe we'd stand a chance!"

Then comes revolt from the rear; dark voices style their way into debate:

"Did you get that ingratitude? And my man was the one who got em up the hill—"

"So what? You think them wheat fokes'll ever admit to that?"

Nope, so don't thaw out the laurel wreath, but now's no time to sob. . . . If you ask me, the driver ought to coast down shortcut Allen Overpass so as to wind up nearer to my own transfer stop to Mia's school in the Haight, and I won't apologize for this personal point of view—there's a hundred me-first stories on this bus and mine is only one. We're only two and a half miles away from the #77 that I'll transfer to in order to pick up the Chick from Lotus Primary School, though I'd planned to stop by home to drop off this ton of welfare forms and proofs of existence yet as ever I've got my itinerary plotted down to a hair of the minute, due to inbuilt saharan sundial beneath rushing timex civ. Hell, with luck we could chug eight miles in no time down winding one-way Allen Pass— It's next to a cliff and a drop, but it's railed on one side and it's not that hedged-in narrow compared to some squeezeplays I've seen and driven; so come on driver, decide to take Allen. There's less than an hour to get Mia from her school where teachers take off promptly at 3:15 and I don't blame em, only hope the Chick remembers to wait inside the building, far away from old mother muggard's.

But which way is this bus going to go? Through the window beside me I look toward Allen Overpass, hump-curved and tight beside its view of dizzy mid-afternoon San Spancisco hills pocked with pinpoints of movement in far-off windows under gunmetal skies. To the west over the ocean is an opaque curtain of vacuum fog hanging in a holding pattern, poised for twilight roll-in-to scoop up our folly and dish it back to sea. I'm struck by the efficiency of the strato-sphere, sitting in patience like a big grey watchgull on our nest of fruit loops below—non-judgmental, returning responsibly day after day, never saying *What next?* or anything of the kind, just hovering contented, nuzzling us all to her big hoary bosom, even our aberoes and recalled products, including me in recall reverie.

I'm lying on the new apartment floor last month with eyes dripping toward onto hardwood boards when comes the thought, sharp as a shard: You know you could have two Mia's and no Muz to pass you breadcrumbs from time to time. You could be living a block away in the Hillmore District around the corner with two hungry Mia's, one a newborn with bottle and hourly diapers. You could be last-ditch needy and you could be handicapped, or with one or more handicapped kids crippled by shriveled pocketbook and toxic habitat. Or worst of all, you could be home in Saint Lou, where Muz is lying in wait, just trying to help in your loss of solid homebase.

"So what do we do?" blurts the busstranger beside me. "Get out and push, all of us?"

"What did I do to deserve this?" someone asks.

The busstranger laughs. "You're speaking a language they don't understand."

But when will the bus go? And where? *Come on driver, make a move!* And he does, up in front he's radioing in as passengers shift, looking loudly at watches held high while in projected escape I glance at the window and look, here comes a schoolkid headed for home, which means the Chick must be out of school already and waiting. Maybe I should give up on this bus, just take off on foot and say fuck it, but that'd be stupid, me loping uphill dragged by weight of this totebag of books and papers and burdensome personal gravity. I'd be moving backward one step for each step forward making my way with progressive regression, a ludicrous image bringing to mind my first witnessed drunk back in kidhood Saint

Brew, our 'cross-the-street neighbor stumbling home once upon a folly-filled night. . . . Through the snow he went toward his porch just ahead. Up two steps, dumdidee dumdidee . . . now bloop bloop bloop—back three. . . .

In any event I won't worry til I'm consternated further; Mia knows better than to set off on her own; she'd never hit the streets on a humbug, her mama didn't raise no fools! We've rehearsed crisis procedure plenty of times and the Chick always passes the test. At four she knows the score enough to be able to shy away instinctively from beckoning danger, so just give her credit, I say to myself— Just think of what's best and have faith in providence, in progeny too. . . . I'm so convinced after this that I smile for a minute, til my breath's caught in sudden forewarning from out of the black, there's a taste of salty wet slime in the back of my throat and Where am I? Who am I? Why am I here among strangers who couldn't care less for my fears and my tears and won't brace me a bit? A child's cry, a blues wail, a moan from the gutter beside me, inside me . . . disjunctive delirium washes over me in waves for an earthly forever, a flinch of eternity—

But movement develops beside me causing me to crash back to Now be here, come in clear. *What's happening with this bus?* There go a few riders marching out the front exit, snatching transfers from the busdriver's pad as they go since he's stepped outside on an unknown mission—maybe checking for needed repair, only to spend ten minutes in feigned *What can I say?* of no move at all, a stall for more time. No matter to him, with bus or busless, with passengers placid or bitter. What does he care if we fret and then mutiny? He gets no combat pay or fool-taming fringes to compensate for our discontent. . . . But wait, he's back at the helm again now, fooling with knobs of his cockpit surrounded by bus ads like

Thunderbolt Temporary Services Has Immediate Openings!
Regular Placements! Top Pay! All Assignments 100% Free!
What Does This Cost You?
NOTHING!

Sure, just temp for a while til you carve out your niche, comes the thought, practical, concrete, and universal-jointed, so that it fits standard fortune *desiderata* exactly, no junkmail dreams attached. *You could hack a stint like this for six months or so, til you grab something better. Be a light traveler, proceeding to heed opportunity's tred.*

But more riders troop past and now I see swelled ranks of schoolkids trudging toward the bus, which makes me decide to set out on foot afterall— My load can be adjusted, no big thing. Hell, there goes a woman up ahead with two toddlers and a grocery bag. I can lay my burden down when I get there to pick up the Chick. Wait, hold it . . . what's this? The sound of engine roar, and the driver gunning his accelerator in glee, or so it seems to everyone including me so that a sprinkle of applause is heard, layered onto static of two-way radio. Then "Ok everybody," the driver grins, "all systems go!" And he warns of intent to zip down Allen Overpass to avoid hills and hassle of oncoming traffic in our state of malaise. A tow truck will meet us at the intersection to Muni

#6, #66, #71, and #77, on the road to success, which sounds good to me. This driver can drive, this coach can coast the curve, and there's trouble-shoot redemption waiting on the other side!